The Illuminati Protocol

ROBERT J. RISTINO

ISBN: 1507872739
ISBN 13: 9781507872734
Library of Congress Control Number: 2015902055
CreateSpace Independent Publishing Platform
North Charleston, South Carolina

DEDICATION

To my daughter, Gaelin, and her dog, Bailey, whose love of family inspired this book.

ACKNOWLEDGEMENTS

While this book has been rattling around in my brain for a number of years it would never have never seen the light of day without the support, guidance and advice of many. First, I want to thank my dear friends and our travel companions, Marita and Wayne Zifcak. Marita did a remarkable and painstaking proofing and critiquing of the initial draft and Wayne took the time away from his semi-retirement to read and comment on the story line. My thanks to long-time friend and colleague, Jim Peters, who reviewed and critiqued the initial draft. I also thank my oldest daughter, Laurie, for her thoughtful critique. Naturally, I must express my appreciation to my wife, Mary, who demonstrated her infinite patience and support by allowing me the time and the space to write. Lastly, and most importantly, I owe a debt of gratitude to my youngest daughter, Gaelin, canine lover extraordinaire, who was first to read the draft, to encourage its publication and to ensure that I got the dogs right.

PROLOGUE

Mahmood ibn Abadi stood sipping a tumbler of 1985 Glenrothes, staring out at the azure blue of the Khor Al Bateen. To his right, he could see Nareel Island. On the left, he could glimpse the marina where lay moored his 40-foot yacht.

As Mahmood slowly savored the amber liquid he was reminded that this was another of the Qur'an commandments that he had broken. Of course, this was the least egregious. Yes, it was har´am. As written in the Qur'an, "an abomination of Shaitan's handiwork." Though a small abomination, for he had committed far more abominable sins than violation of the proscription on alcohol. So he knew that Allah would condemn him long before that sin, on the tally sheet of his life, came before The Almighty. That thought did little to ease his mind. And so, he gratefully poured himself another half tumbler of scotch.

His momentary idle was broken by the jar of the intercom. "You have a call, sayyed," the pleasant voice said. "A Samir Sarief. Should I put him through?"

"Yes," he said hesitantly, "but give me a moment, please."

He preferred not taking Sarief's call. He knew that it would cause him undo anxiety and consternation. But one must do what one must do. As Senior Managing Director for Wealth Management at the International Bank of the Emirates, Mahmood often had to soil his hands with unpleasantness. And this call he knew would involve a high degree of unpleasantness.

Sarief had the unenviable role of fronting for one of the richest Sheikhs in the Emirates, a Sheikh who had a personal account in the IBE of nearly 300 million US. For the IBE, he was more than a whale. The Sheikh was a pod of whales and Mahmood treated him as such. The question was – what did he want?

With some trepidation Mahmood picked up the phone, turning an anxiety riddled psyche into a confident, professional tone. "Allo, my friend. So how may I help you today?"

"So good to hear your voice once again Mahmood," Sareif responded cheerily. "Naturally, I am about my master's business. It concerns a highly personal and sensitive matter. It is business best conducted in complete privacy. Perhaps the Cinnabar at the Hilton, at four this afternoon? You know the Cinnabar?"

"Yes, I know it. At four, hmm … well I think that is manageable. Always good to meet with you, my friend." Mahmood paused for a moment before asking, "Can you give me any idea what the Sheikh might want from us?"

"We'll talk this afternoon. Much better to discuss it then. See you at four."

■ ■ ■

Far from prying eyes, Mahmood sat back in his chair to the far right of the enormous, elliptical-shaped bar with its retro diner barstools. The spacious lounge had a purpled hue, a symbiotic result of the lighting and wall treatments. He played nervously with the collar of his kandura, the popular, knee length shirt worn by most male Emirati.

Trying to relax, he focused on John Coltrane's "Body and Soul" played live by a Chicago jazz ensemble. The group performed on a stage that stood above and in back of the enormous bar.

He waited anxiously, slowly sipping a 16-year-old Lagavulin from a teacup. He hoped that the smoky liquid would calm him. He preferred his Glenrothes. Unfortunately, they were out of it. So he generously acquiesced to a Lagavulin, whose exotic mix of fruitcake with sweet seaweed overtones was a delicious compromise. The attractive and astute waitress had thoughtfully provided the scotch in a teacup with saucer. It would avoid drawing unnecessary attention from the more observant Muslims among the patrons.

The bank executive had become enamored of scotch whiskies while studying for his advanced degree in international finance at the London School of Economics. Two of his classmates, one a Brit and the other Irish, introduced him to the intoxicating liquor. All three had remained good friends and that relationship had proven very advantageous for Mahmood.

Cinnabar was among the most elegant nightclubs in Abu Dhabi. Unfortunately, the kind of people who frequented the Cinnabar were from the same circle of glitterati as Mahmood and his wife Jamillah. So Mahmood fretted about being seen. He'd rather get this meeting over with. Leave and arrange to meet his surriyya at the flat he paid for at the Arthuryeeda.

Dominique was lovely and very, very expensive. French, with a fetish for clothes, jewelry and pleasing Mahmood in so many exotic ways. Ways that his wife could never imagine, much less do. It was a typical indulgence of men of his class.

Was such behavior another abominable sin? Zina – intercourse outside of marriage – was a sin but not if committed with a concubine – a surriyya. Was Dominque a surriyya? No, not in the full sense of the word. But Mahmood knew that he was a zaani – a fornicator.

These random thoughts evaporated into the warm air of the Cinnabar as Samir came into view. Short, wiry, well dressed with skin and hair glistening with an oily sheen, to which the purpled lighting gave a deathly hue. His face reminded Mahmood of a hawk, all nasty with purpose and little, if any, emotion.

Mahmood rose and extended his hand. "As-salam alaykum."

Samir took his hand shaking it vigorously. "Wa alakum as-salam."

Mahmood gestured for him to sit, a teacup of Lagavulin set before him.

Samir carefully fingered the teacup. "My dear Mahmood, you always know how to get a meeting off on the right foot, as the English say." He slowly sipped, a smile crossing his face. "Absolutely lovely *tea*."

"We both suffer from the same frailty, a love of good *tea*," Mahmood said, tipping his glass toward Samir in a silent toast.

Samir sipped the well-aged scotch, rolling it gently over his tongue. As he swallowed, a bright grin spread across his rather narrow face. He licked his lips slowly as he lowered the teacup to the table.

"Well, well Mahmood, you are looking prosperous. I imagine business has been good for you and the IBE."

"Yes, good. Very good, in fact. The international downturn was, for us, a remarkable opportunity to buy and invest in some very lucrative markets," he responded, wishing that Samir would just get on with it and stop this charade of making chit-chat. "Yes, I must say, we've done very well for ourselves, our investors and our clients, the Sheikh foremost among them."

"Indeed. The Sheikh has been very pleased with his returns of late and how you have managed his portfolio. You've done very well by the Sheikh and he has done very well by you. No?"

"Yes, the Sheikh has been most kind. So how can I further assist him?"

Samir waved a dismissive hand in the air.

"In a moment, my dear Mahmood, in a moment. I want to spend a few minutes catching up. How about that lovely daughter of yours? Baseema, the smiling one, isn't it? How is she doing at the London School of Economics? She's in her second year now, I think?"

"Well, yes," Mahmood responded guardedly. "... but how did you know about Baseema. I never mentioned my daughter to you."

"Like you, Mahmood, I am a businessman. As such, I try to know everything I can about those with whom I share business interests with and," he smiled gently, "since I have no family of my own, I fill my life with thoughts of the families of those I both admire and respect."

Mahmood eyed him cautiously. "I appreciate both your concern and interest in my family, Samir."

Mahmood sat staring at Samir for a moment wondering what he was playing at. Why the mention of his family? A veiled threat perhaps? If so, why? This arrangement of theirs was, after all, simply business. Nothing more.

"So why is that?" Mahmood inquired. "Why is it that you have no wife, no children?"

"I have never had the good fortune to meet a woman such as your lovely Jamillah. If that had been the case, I would have tied the nuptial knot years ago. As for children, for all I know, I may have fathered many, who knows," he laughed.

Raising his teacup, Mahmood offered a toast. "May you have the good fortune someday to meet a woman as fair, as good and as devoted as my Jamillah."

"Thank you, Mahmood. You are a fortunate man that, when this meeting ends, you will have a lovely woman to return to. Though, tell me, will you go directly home or by way of the Arthuryeeda on Haaza Bin Zayed?"

For just a moment Mahmood was taken aback, his face flushing. Samir immediately saw the fear in his host's eyes, waving his hand in a reassuring gesture.

"Not to worry, my friend. Your private life is safe with me, but do be careful. For if I know your secrets others may also."

Mahmood quickly downed what remained of his scotch and then gestured for the waitress to refill both their teacups.

"As you say, my private life is of no one's concern but my own," he uttered with as little emotion as possible. "I expect that as a close business associate you will keep this little piece of information private."

Samir bowed his head in obeisance. "So... to business then?"

"Yes, of course. What is it that the Sheikh needs of me?"

Mahmood had not been surprised by the request. He had made similar arrangements for the Sheikh in the past.

Nevertheless, this was a part of his job that he found extremely distasteful and, somewhat, chilling.

Since both he and Samir had engaged in similar transactions, little had to be said except for the business aspects of the arrangements. Samir merely passed along a slip of paper to Mahmood with the terse explanation, "These are the specifications. No deviations."

They then briefly discussed a delivery date and the all-important price. The package, Samir insisted, must be delivered undamaged within a month of order placement. While the Sheikh would be billed $1.25 million for the order, Mahmood would only receive $1 million. The other quarter of a million was Samir's cut or what he called "carrying charges." After Mahmood took his 10 percent off the top, that left the banker with $900,000 to procure the package.

After Samir made his excuses and left, Mahmood opened the sheet of paper. In a neat scrawl, Samir had written:

Caucasian, English speaking female, height 4'6"-5', appropriate weight for height, light complexion, blue eyes, blond hair with lovely facial features between 9 and 11 years of age. Must be a virgin, totally free of any skin blemishes, deformities or handicaps.

1

Lyle Stembeck eased himself into the passenger seat of his SUV. In his lap was a Nikon Digital SLR with a 200mm lens. A very good camera he was fond of telling those he could tell. Set him back $1100. But that was the price of doing business. And this was business.

He brought the Nikon up to his right eye, scanning the playground. A couple of minutes and it would be recess. Ah, there they were. Fourth graders out to play. Now to find her in the crowd. Need some good pics. *K* always insisted on seeing and approving the product before he'd give the go ahead. A very fussy man. As much for business, Lyle thought, as it was for pleasure.

It didn't take him long to find her. She was a knockout or would soon be, although only about 10 or 11. She fit the buyer's specs perfectly. Long, very blond hair, pretty Caucasian features, svelte figure, nice legs and a cute butt for someone so young. She was wearing a pink sweater over a short plaid skirt with dark red leggings and sneakers. Could be Adidas or Nikes, he thought. Fleetingly, he wondered who the buyer was. Probably some wealthy pervert Saudi Sheikh or Brunei prince. No matter, they paid on time and they paid well. Or at least, *K* paid on time and paid well.

He congratulated himself on the find. It had only taken him a week. But now came the hard part. Acquisition of intelligence, abduction plan, execution and delivery. So, to quote Eli Wallach in the Magnificent Seven, "To business."

Lyle opened the camera's memory chip compartment and removed the old chip replacing it with a new 8 GB. Peering at the Nikon's 3" view screen, he scanned the playground until he saw her. Adjusting focus, he held down the on/off button. The camera slowly whirred as it began taking one frame after another. He checked the view screen to preview the shots. There were 20 or so, more than adequate for government work, as Lyle liked to say. He took a cable and attached it to the camera, inserting the other end into his smartphone. He speed dialed *K*, downloading all the photos. Have fun, you perv'.

Step one complete. Now he dismantled the camera and lens, placing them in their carrying cases. Starting the engine he began thinking of step two – intelligence acquisition – identifying where she lived.

■ ■ ■

When *K* received the photos he was delighted. Just what the client appeared to want. Perfect in every way. However, it was the client who would make the final decision. So *K* went into the deep web to a site few had ever seen and fewer still could enter. The *Enlightened Ones* site was buried so deep in the cyberspace that it would be nearly impossible to find without specific instructions.

Once in, he posted the photo file to the requesting party. Now he would just have to wait. Within hours he had his decision. It was a GO! With the confirmatory order he also received the amount to be paid once the package was delivered – a cool $250,000. God, this guy must really trip out on young, sweet little pussy.

K immediately phoned Lyle with the good news. While Lyle was ecstatic he also felt the enormous pressure of having to execute this abduction in matter of a few days. This particular order, *K* had said, was very time sensitive. Lyle figured whoever placed the order must have one huge hard-on for this little cutie.

2

Lyle was quite proud of himself. Mostly because of this aspect of the planning process – intelligence acquisition.

He was not your common, everyday child abductor, and there were many, far more than people realized, who rarely planned an abduction. Child abduction was most often a crime of opportunity. Child left unattended at the right place, wrong time, and bang, gone. Happened a lot. Of course, these abductions were the crimes of sociopathic pedophiles. Lyle believed he was neither a sociopath nor a pedophile.

During one of his low points – when a dark mood would come over him with that heavy-chest feeling squeezing his ribs like a vice – Lyle would spend hours researching his *condition*. He learned that as a man attracted to post-pubescent females, he was not a pedophile. He was what the psychologists called an ephebopheliac. He liked that word. He liked being an ephebopheliac. Just a guy who felt more comfortable with adolescent girls. They kept him feeling young, vibrant, alive – and with such young girls he was always in control, sexually, socially, intellectually.

With that bit of self-discovery, Lyle felt relieved, somehow cleansed. He wasn't a pervert, a pedophile, a child rapist. He was no *K*! Just a guy who liked them young. After all, what man didn't? Now, he could see himself as simply a professional who just happened to abduct children as a business.

To prove the point to himself and others in the trade, he pointed to his girlfriend, or at least the latest one. True, some of them had been rather young, like Mandy who was just 14. But, as Lyle explained, she was a fully mature woman, quite receptive to his sexual advances. She was a runaway. He had picked her up on the highway and saved her from life on the streets. She proved to be more than grateful. He gave her a nice place to live, food, expensive clothes and jewelry, booze, and occasional drugs. And she gave him sex – lots of sex – and adoration.

If you pushed him, he'd admit that he had had intercourse with some younger girls, including two of his abductees, but that was before *K* and the whole Illuminati thing. They insisted, or *K* did, that the product be left untouched, virginal. Touch the product and you'd lose an appendage, the one between your legs. That was the primary protocol. That's what *K* called the rules – protocols.

K had taken some time explaining the Illuminati network's protocols. These rules were inviolate. They defined the business aspect of the network's child sex trafficking business line. First and foremost, deliver the product to the customer as specified in the order. Secondly, whenever possible, avoid harming anyone – including the product – during any phase of the order fulfillment process (not, *K* emphasized, because of any moral compunction but rather as an effort to avoid excessive law enforcement involvement). Thirdly, if taken into custody for any reason, await contact by network assigned legal counsel. Fourth, any network member who cooperates with law enforcement agencies involved in the investigation of network activities will suffer *extreme sanction* (*K* said this was a euphemism for a bullet in the head!). Fifth, fees were pre-set by the network, non-negotiable, and would be paid by non-traceable wire transfer between a network offshore subsidiary bank and an offshore bank of the contractor's choice. Sixth, individual members of the network shall only have knowledge and communication with the member above and below them in the distribution chain. Lastly, there is no retirement plan (another euphemism, *K* explained, since you couldn't retire from the network but the network could retire you!).

If it weren't for the money – and the money was great – Lyle would have told *K* to shove his protocols up his ass. But the money spoke louder than Lyle's personal annoyance, so he zipped his mouth shut and stopped diddling his victims.

Beyond the issue of his sexual proclivities, Lyle was also sensitive to the moral ambiguity surrounding his line of work. As hard as he thought to understand his sexual preferences, he worked harder still justifying what he did as an avocation. Lyle refused to think of himself as evil. In fact, he thought of himself as quite a superior man, better than most. It was a social psychology course in community college that gave him the essential insight that he needed. His raison d'etre was really quite simple and, therefore, elegant.

In the course, the instructor introduced the students to the concept of Social Darwinism. According to its tenets, the professor explained, some people were born to exploit and others to be exploited. Very simple, really. Those who were stronger, more intelligent and more unscrupulous would survive and dominate society and they should – the strong survive and the weak perish. The survivors were the doers, the masters, the leaders, the scions, the rulers, the predators. And he, Lyle, was one of them.

When he had laid all this out for *K*, the man looked into his eyes astonished, "Lyle, stop masturbating because I think you're overworking your brain."

Nevertheless, Lyle was unperturbed. Social Darwinism was a good theory. It worked for him and that's all that mattered.

■ ■ ■

For Lyle, stage one of intelligence acquisition was scouting the school grounds. He needed a relatively concealed spot from where he could observe the front entrance of the school as the children boarded their busses at the end of the school day. The front of the school faced a street that led directly to downtown.

Behind the school, there was an old railroad bed fronted by a 14-foot-high berm. The railroad bed dated back to the 19th century, during a period when all these small New England towns were connected by a labyrinthine network of rails. The berm was now overgrown with bushes, oak, maple, and pine. Perfect for concealment.

Lyle drove around to the other side of the school where a road ran perpendicular to the road fronting the school. He parked his van in a small, overgrown, empty lot. It was just a short walk into the woods. The abandoned rail bed had been kept clear of debris and brush. It was being used as a walking path for locals to enjoy the area's flora and fauna. Very convenient for them, but also troublesome. Someone could accidentally stumble on him if they just looked casually to their left, along the top of the berm. He pulled a pad and pen out of his jacket pocket and jotted a note: *cover story needed.*

He walked along the path for about 100 yards, then climbed the berm. He hadn't quite cleared the rear of the school. He walked another 50 yards, pushing his way through the brush to the berm's edge. Yes, this was the spot. Perfect. From here he could see the front entrance clearly. Good cover too.

A *ra-tat-tat* caused him to quickly look up. Must be a woodpecker. There it was. Atop a rotting pine. It was a Pileated. The largest of the woodpeckers. A veritable airborne wrecking crew. That would be his cover story.

Lyle had used the bird watching cover before. Very effective. A couple of years ago he had bought some guidebooks – *Birds of America* and *The Sibley Guide to Birds* – both of which he studied assiduously. He also created a personal birders journal filled with numerous notes and sketches of fictitious sightings. Lyle carried his journal, guidebooks, and binoculars in a haversack swung over his shoulder – standard accouterment for a birder – whenever a cover story was needed.

Only once had his cover story nearly backfired on him. He had been scouting a small playground where quite a few local kids congregated after school. A thick wood surrounded the playground. He had positioned himself on a small knoll at the tree line when he felt a gentle tapping on his shoulder. He turned quickly around nearly herniating a cervical disc. Staring at him was this incredibly homely woman.

"Have you happened to have spotted a Snowy Owl in your search today?" she asked in a barely audible voice.

"No," Lyle responded attempting to keep both angst and irritation out of his voice.

"Oh, sorry to bother." She gestured to the other two women and the two men standing behind her. "We're all with the local Audubon Chapter. Heard that someone had spotted one near here. Rather rare in the daytime."

"Sorry, can't help you."

"See anything interesting? Other than us, of course," she said smiling at her own joke.

"No, you're the best I've done today."

"Well, we always like to meet other birders. It's nearly one, and we're all headed to the diner in town for a bite. Would you care to join us?" An offer the group seemed enthusiastic about. Lyle was beginning to think that they weren't a group of serial birders but a Christian Singles group.

"What a nice offer, but I really have to get going. Much to do and much to see."

"We understand," she sounded disappointed, her hawkish nose giving her the look of a bird of prey, as she held a card out to him. "Here is my card. Do contact us if you'd like to join our group on one of our weekly excursions. We're really a lot of fun."

There were nods of agreement from the other birders with hands fluttering to quietly wave goodbye.

"I'm sure you are. I'll give it some thought if I'm in the neighborhood again," NOT, he thought to himself. He got up, flung his haversack over his shoulder and waved to the group as he hurriedly exited the woods. "Fuckin' birders," he whispered.

The homely one waved to him with the expression of a predator that had just missed its meal.

Here in these woods, should anyone ask, he would be in search of the elusive dryocopus pileatus – the pileated woodpecker. The cover story worked well with his day job, operating a small photo studio. He made a decent living but it was the money he earned abducting for the Illuminati that was funding his long sought retirement.

■ ■ ■

It was early Saturday evening. He would return early on Monday morning to set up. The plan was simple. He would surveil the front entrance during student drop-off to identify the target's bus. Take note of the bus number. Return in the afternoon when the busses queued up to deliver students home.

On Monday, he took up his position at his observation post. His powerful binoculars strapped around his neck. His Nikon sat atop his haversack next to his right leg. The busses began arriving precisely on schedule, dumping the children off. He watched carefully for some 10 minutes before spotting her.

A different outfit -- a blue jumper over pale blue tights. He carefully scanned the bus waiting for it to pull out of queue so he could get a full view of it. He began taking photos of the bus with his 200 mm telephoto lens, though photos weren't necessary since he could plainly see the number on the side of the bus – 24.

He wrapped up his gear, trotted down to his SUV, packed up and drove over to Buxton, just a few miles from Wilton. There he found a diner for a spot of lunch. He parked in the rear.

After lunch, he returned to his SUV, entered the back seat, and took off his pants and shirt revealing a cycling outfit. He quickly changed into cycling shoes, a pair of silver-tinted sunglasses, and a Tour d'France cap. From the rear of the SUV, he rolled out a Raleigh 16-speed touring bike.

He cycled down to an intersection about a quarter of a mile from the school. He had observed that all of the busses exited the school parking lot by turning right onto School Street. At the intersection, each bus began to take a different direction, depending on the route it ran. The busses could either go left, right or straight ahead. He sat on his bike waiting at the intersection in the small parking lot of a package store. Ironic, he thought, states pass laws forbidding the selling of drugs within a specified area around schools but then allow a liquor store right down the street. Go figure.

Six, seven, eight busses passed by before he spotted number 24. It turned left. He let it get 100 yards or so in front, before he began tailing. After about a quarter of a mile, the bus began to make frequent stops, disgorging an ever-changing number of kids. The younger ones greeted by their parent, while the older kids seemed to slowly drift back along the roadway, appearing in no apparent hurry to reach home, or anywhere else for that matter.

The bus was slowly making its way down a heavily treed road that bore a sign that read "Scenic Road." He kept a good distance from the bus. When it stopped, he veered toward the right hand side of the road so that he could see what children were getting off. When a fork appeared in the road ahead, the bus went to the right, around a curve and up a steep hill. Along this hilly stretch of road, it continued to disgorge students for another 15 minutes.

The route took the bus past a small Lutheran church, then under power lines around a curve and down a hill, where the bus slowed up and took a right. The road here had both an entrance and exit divided by a small brick wall that bore the legend "Ledgemere Way."

Almost immediately after making the turn, the bus stopped and five children exited. The last one was the target. Three of the children were picked up by their suburban soccer moms who hustled them off into their cars. The other older two, the target, and another girl – friend perhaps – began walking up a steep road that paralleled Ledgemere Way.

Lyle had intentionally passed the bus when it began to slow up to stop. He pulled his bike over to the side of the road. He knelt by the bike feigning a close examination of his bicycle chain. He saw the target exit the bus and begin walking up the hill. He remounted his bike, made a U-turn and went back down the hill. Turning behind the bus he peddled up the steep road about 30 yards behind the two girls.

On the hill, he switched to a much lower gear, beginning a slow, upward climb, taking his time. Luckily, the target stopped in front of the second house on the hill road. She waved good-bye to her friend, then danced along the driveway into the house's garage. The number on the mailbox read 20 Rockridge Road.

Just as he was about to crest the hill, he looked back, noticing the girl re-merge from the garage and sprint down the side of the hill. He stopped momentarily to watch her. She turned left, crossing another yard to the rear porch of a house that fronted the main road. She talked to someone on the porch and a moment later two dogs came bounding outside.

Lyle didn't want to press his luck so he pushed off. It took him 10 minutes to return to his SUV.

Now that he had her address, time to go hunting.

3

Peggy Laughlin, the Wilton Police duty sergeant, sat rhythmically tapping her fingers on the desk. Where was he, she kept thinking? Her headaches would start if she didn't get her caffeine fix soon. Gerry had one simple thing to do. Pick up the friggin' coffee at the BrewHouse. Simple enough, but evidently too much for Gerry. Dumb shit.

That thought stayed with her only a nanosecond before the front door swung open. Gingerly balancing a tray of coffees, Officer Gerry Spiller stepped in.

"Hi all," he said.

"Get over here," Peggy yelled.

"Chill, Serge. I'm only a couple of minutes late."

"Couple of minutes, my ass," she said, grabbing for her double-shot café latte.

Gerry rolled his eyes.

"Hey, how about me!"

Gerry turned to see Chief Arnie Cook standing in his office doorway waving him over.

The chief took his coffee, gesturing to an empty desk in the center of the floor. "You better just leave those. Fric and Frac are out seeing to a fender bender on Jefferson."

The coffee saga ended abruptly when the 911-response system phone rang. Peggy answered.

"Wilton Police Department, Sergeant Lawlor speaking. What is your emergency?"

"My daughter is missing," a very nervous male voice said.

"Please identify yourself."

"My name is Matthew Gaines. I mean, we live at 20 Rockridge Road."

"OK, Mr. Gaines, now what are your daughter's name, age and description?"

"Please just come. We're wasting time here."

"Don't worry, we'll have an officer there momentarily," Peggy said in a voice as calm and controlled as she could manage. "But I do need this information."

"Her name is Katherine. We call her Katie. She's 11 years old. About…" he dropped off line for a moment then came back on. "Umm, she's about 4'10", 74 lbs., long, light blond hair, blue/green eyes and fair complexion," he explained haltingly as someone in the background fed him the description.

"And when did you find her missing?" Peggy asked thinking the man sounded extremely distraught.

"About six o'clock, when we went to wake her for school."

"OK, Mr. Gaines. We're dispatching a police officer immediately. Please stay in your home until she arrives."

"Yes, we'll be here. Please hurry."

Peggy hung up the 911 phone. "Chief, we got a missing person 911 over on Rockridge. Trish is on patrol, I'll have her respond."

The Chief looked up. "Get a hold of Fric and Frac and when they finish with their fender bender have them report to Trish at the Rockridge address. Hey, who is the family?"

"Will do! 'Gaines,' chief. That's their name."

"Hmm. Gaines, don't know them. Hope it isn't anything more than a runaway."

She looked back at the chief, two minds with but a single thought.

■ ■ ■

Special Agent Bing Ingram stood staring at the 12-year-old case file. His head propped on closed fists pressed firmly to his cheeks. It was his monthly act of contrition – the victim he didn't recover, the case he didn't solve. He had promised them – something he should never have done – but he had, promised them that he would find her. Now, once a month, he'd review Samantha George's file just to remind himself that she was out there and that he had unfinished business with those who had taken her.

Samantha was a lovely little girl of 10 when she went missing. With silky milk chocolate skin, mounds of dark wavy hair and those big brown eyes, she gave promise of the beauty that she was destined to become. The child of a dark-skinned

Caribbean model and a local tennis pro, Sammi had gone missing from their home on a Tuesday night, never to be seen again.

The FBI agent had been a member of the Northeast Regional Child Abduction Rapid Deployment team since the team's establishment in 2006. For the last eight, its leader. The CARD teams specialized in abduction cases. If the person missing was 12 or under, it was their case to be had. George had been one of his early cases. Since then he had had a perfect recovery record. But her case was the one he dwelled on – the one that stuck in his throat like a piece of cud.

Ingram was highly respected, not only for his outstanding recovery record, but also his tenacious and astute fieldwork. A U.S. Army veteran who had served in Desert Storm in the CID, he had joined the FBI following his discharge. Since then he had earned a doctoral degree in forensic psychology and undergone extensive special training at Quantico in crimes against children. His educational background made him a natural for the Behavioral Analysis Unit but he preferred serving in a CARD team. He felt it more professionally rewarding or, perhaps, because he had children of his own.

Nationally, Ingram had a well-earned reputation as an expert in the field of child abduction. The Bureau had him teach a course once a year at Quantico where he also served as a special consultant to the National Center for Analysis of Violent Crimes. Boston University had also recruited him to teach part-time in their Criminal Justice program. He was highly thought of at BU and had been offered a full-time gig as an associate professor. He had turned it down.

His students thought him quirky, but fought to get into his oversubscribed courses. In fact, some in the Bureau thought he appeared more professorial than professional. Partly, he knew, because of his rather idiosyncratic manner of dress. He had an ensemble that could only be charitably described as mid-fifties – brown felt Australian bush hat, worn tweed jackets, bow ties, plaid vests, baggy corduroy pants and heavy duty hiking boots. He was his own man, especially when it came to his wardrobe. Of course, there was method to his sartorial choices as there was always method to whatever he did.

"Where were you, Sammi and who had taken you?" The questions he kept voicing in his head over and over again for the past 12 years. While there had been some clues, the modus operandi had been clear enough, but all led to nothing. Leads dried up quickly. No one had seen or heard anything. There was no request for ransom. No body ever turned up. Nothing. Not a friggin' thing. She had just evaporated like morning mist into the cool, crisp autumn air. "Where were you, Sammi and who had taken you?"

As the question lingered, his office door swung open. "Bingo, looks like we've caught one." Tall and lithe, Special Agent Alexandra Dabrowski stood before him with a piece of paper in her hand. She handed it to him. "An 11-year-old girl went missing in Wilton."

"Where?" Bing asked.

"Wilton, Mass."

"Where the hell is Wilton?"

"West of here about 40 miles, as the bird flies."

Bing scanned the missing person's report from the NCIC advisory. "OK, Ola, better saddle up the team. Lets be ready to rock n' roll in 10 minutes," he looked up at Ola, "and let the locals know that the cavalry is coming."

4

Officer Trish D'Amadeo made a quick U-turn on Main Street after receiving Peggy's call. She flicked her patrol car lights and siren on, heading back downtown figuring that was the fastest way to the Rockridge sub division. It had started as a beautiful fall day. The sun was bright; the cloudless sky a crystalline topaz blue. Now this.

While only 27, she had already made sergeant and was highly thought of by Chief Cook. Even her fellow male officers held her in high regard. She was a no nonsense, forthright, hard working, competent police officer and everyone respected that. They all liked her – the sister they never had or wished they had.

Of course, her acceptance into the local male-dominated police fraternity didn't happen over night. It took a while. At 5'7', 135 pounds, small waisted, a butt that you could serve drinks on, curly, sienna colored hair, and an oval Modigliani face to die for, she had been told more than once by those of both sexes that she was a knockout. The two-inch scar over her right cheekbone only seeming to enhance rather than detract from her good looks. In private, even Fric and Frac had admitted that no one filled out a police uniform the way Trish did.

Unfortunately, she didn't know if being attractive was a benefit or a hindrance to career advancement. It had presented more than a few problems while she was serving in the military. She had handled those encounters well, at least that was what her superior officers had said, even though, at times, some of them were the problem.

■ ■ ■

Trish had come to the department only two years ago, following graduation from the Massachusetts State Police Academy. She entered the academy after a deployment to Afghanistan with a U.S. Army Military Police unit. She was a member of a cadre of MPs stationed in a small village 30 clicks south of Kabul, training Afghanis in policing and counterterrorism. It was what she liked to call an interesting growth experience, but one fraught with some frightening memories.

Whenever anyone asked her about her Afghani experience Trish tried to downplay it. While she had avoided a full bout of PTSD, her experience had left her with emotional scars that were still raw. Thinking about it only brought her back to the afternoon when she lost a good friend and three of her fellow officers.

It was lunchtime. Captain Joann Sullivan was sitting across from her in the small, tin-roofed hut that passed for a mess hall. The heat was stifling. Some one had purloined the only fan. So they cooled off by drinking chilled Budweiser and rubbing the cans across the tops of their now glistening chests. They were chatting about their favorite subject – the weaker, dumber sex.

"But I tell you, Trish," she threw a hand over to her left, "Captain Cocksman over there, I bet he's a good bang."

"What did you call him?"

"Captain Cocksman. I got that from Sergeant Beneventura. She said she got a gander of him coming out of the shower, excuse the pun, and he was hung like a fuckin' stallion. It just about touched the floor!" Joann held her hands a foot apart to demonstrate.

"You're so horny Joann that you'd actually believe that crap? He probably paid Bene to pass along that skinny just to warm our little pussies."

"Well, on behalf of all the women posted to this friggin' shit hole, I'm going to get that guy to screw me and I'll..." It was the last thing she said as an explosion tore apart the mess hall sending shrapnel screaming in every direction. A piece caught Joann just above the left ear driving four inches into her brain and killing her instantly. Blood flew from her skull, spraying a fine crimson mist over Trish's face. Three others were also killed, all sitting behind Joann and Trish, and 23 wounded.

It happened so quickly and the adrenaline rush so intense, that Trish hadn't realized that she was among the injured. Most of the blood that covered her face, arms and chest, wasn't Joann's – it was hers. While conscious, she couldn't remember the medics treating her or the air evac to the military hospital in Kabul. She was in surgery for three hours with surgeons removing seven pieces of shrapnel. One of the surgeons told her that anyone of those pieces, if it had hit the right spot, could have killed her. She had been one lucky soldier. Joann had not.

So for her, Afghanistan would always be Joann – funny, horny, and who never got to prove if the cocksman was truly the cock man.

■ ■ ■

Trish was pressing her cruiser to go as fast as prudence would allow, given Wilton's winding streets. She kept thinking of the parents. They must be out of their minds with worry. Have to be calm, reassuring, professional. Keep it together. Review the department's missing person's protocols.

Trish reached over into the passenger's seat, grabbing her iPad Air. She opened it and went to her WPD protocols file. She tapped the document titled "Missing Person." She began reviewing the instructions as best she could, while driving down Main then taking a left on to Williams. Once on Williams, it only took four minutes to get to Rockridge Road.

The Gaines house was the second on the right with a steep driveway that made a gentle left hand curve up to the attached garage. The house was a well-maintained contemporary with a front overhang and a back that appeared to butt up against a ledge outcropping. The outcropping formed the upper part of a ridge. Power lines ran across the top, visible from the street but not the Gaines driveway.

Trish pulled the cruiser in front of the garage. She quickly scanned the protocol one more time. As she exited the cruiser, Gaines and his wife came out the front entrance walking down a brick path to meet her. The wife's eyes were very red. She was an attractive woman, very trim but disheveled. She hadn't bothered to pull herself together. And she looked like the type that always did. She was wearing black slacks with a white blouse buttoned one shy of the collar. Her hair was pulled back into a ponytail and she wore no makeup. The husband was a few inches taller, also trim, pleasant looking and well tanned. He was wearing a pair of dress trousers, and a white dress shirt. They were, all in all, she thought, an attractive suburban couple.

Trish introduced herself, holding out her right hand. The husband took it in his. It was sweaty. The woman remained leaning against her husband. Her arms folded tightly about her chest.

"Officer, I'm Martin Gaines and this is my wife, Ginny." He paused a moment, nervously gesturing to the front door. "We should go in."

Trish followed them into the house. Ginny never undoing her arms. They entered a foyer, then a short flight of steps up to an open living, dining and kitchen space occupying a good portion of the home's second floor. Martin gestured for her to take a seat on the sofa. Trish waved his offer off.

"Do you have any other children," she asked.

"Yes, Marty. He's 9. He's over at our neighbor's house down the street. Didn't want him in the middle of all of this," Ginny explained anticipating Trish's next question.

Trish nodded. "I'll have to speak with him after we finish. Now I first need to search the house. Make sure that she isn't hiding somewhere."

The couple both looked a bit unnerved. "What for?" questioned Martin. "We've been through this place three times. She's not here!" His voice rising with both anger and anxiety.

"I just have to be sure, sir," said Trish apologetically. "Please, could we start with her room?"

He took her down the corridor that ran to the right off of the living room. Katie's room was at the corner of the house on the left at the end of the corridor. Trish followed the husband into the room with the wife right behind her. It was a typical adolescent girl's room; at least that's what Trish thought an adolescent girl's room should look like. It was decorated with various posters, one of Beyoncé exposing her walnut-cracking thighs, and another of Britney Spears. There were two windows, one on the left wall facing the next-door neighbor's house that was barely visible from the window.

The other window was in the same corner of the room but facing the back yard, or what there was of a back yard. Katie's queen-size bed was next to the window. It had been slept in. The wall next to the bed featured a large walk-in closet.

Trish first inspected the windows. The one facing the neighbor was closed with no apparent tampering. The one facing the back was slightly ajar. She also noticed that the outside window screen appeared to have a tear in the lower, right hand corner.

Trish took a pair of plastic gloves out of her back pocket and put them on. She gingerly lifted the window, closely inspecting the tear. It was L-shaped, cut clean along the bottom corner of the window. Large enough for a hand, she thought. She retrieved a small digital camera from her other pocket and took photos of the window screen.

Turning to the couple huddled near her, she pointed to the window screen. "Did either of you notice this tear in the screen before this morning?" They both shook their heads "no".

The husband leaned over to inspect the screen. "Did someone cut this opening? Is that what you're saying?" He sounded agitated.

"I'm not saying anything, sir. I'm just taking a careful look at everything. That's all."

Trish continued a search of the room including looking under the bed.

"What the hell are you looking under the bed for? Didn't you think we'd do that?"

"Just being thorough, sir. You never know what you might find."

The wife grabbed her husband's arm gently, her eyes pleading with him to back off and to keep it together.

The husband appeared to be losing it. The wife was quiet, looking absolutely terrified. After Trish searched the walk-in closet and the bureau, she asked if any clothes were missing. They didn't think so.

Trish then searched a small desk opposite the bed. Nothing much except for school notebooks, a calendar with numerous scribbled notes, and a laptop. "I'll need to take her laptop, just in case there is something in here that may give us a lead as to her whereabouts."

Trish spent the next ten minutes searching the rest of the house. Nothing unusual and no Katie. When they returned to the living room she asked if the Gaines minded answering a few more questions. They nodded, sat down on the sofa and Trish sat in an armchair facing them.

"These questions are all standard for a missing person. But, before we begin, do you have a recent photo of Katie?"

Ginny got up and walked over to the fireplace. She took a photo off the mantle and passed it to Trish. "Will this do? We had that done only about four months ago."

"Great, Thanks." Trish took a picture of Katie's photo with her iPad and emailed it to the chief with a note: *Here's Katie Gaines' most recent photo. Please share with all. Thanks. T.*

When Trish was finished she turned back to the couple. "Has Katie ever run away from home?"

"No, never," Ginny said.

"Does she ever leave the house early to meet up with friends before the school bus arrives?"

"No," Ginny said. "She pretty much always stays to her schedule."

"What schedule is that?"

"She gets up about 6:30. Showers, dresses, sometimes does some last-minute homework in the kitchen. She eats breakfast, often with one or all of us and then she's out the door for the 7:15 bus," Ginny explained.

"No problems with kids at school, issues of bullying or the like?"

"None. She's a great kid. Everyone loves Katie. I mean everyone."

Evidently, someone doesn't, Trish thought. "Does she have a boyfriend?"

"What," Martin interrupted, "a boyfriend at her age. Of course not."

"Just a necessary question that we have to ask, Mr. Gaines. Today, kids grow up fast and can be very precocious. When we finish, could you please give me a list of all her neighborhood and school friends? That would be very helpful."

Trish looked pensive for a moment, scanning the questions on her iPad.

"Tell me, does Katie have any learning or developmental disabilities?"

"No, none," said Ginny. "She's a very bright, young girl, does very well at school and is very athletic. Now it's soccer."

"Sounds like a great kid," Trish acknowledged. "So she's never had any problems at school or here at home?"

"No. I mean, you know, the usual thing for a child her age."

"What do you mean, the 'usual thing,' " Trish asked.

"Oh, getting in fights with her brother, forgetting to put her laundry away. You know, things like that."

"Tell, me, did Katie seem all right to the two of you last night before she went to bed? Was anything bothering her?"

"She was fine. Had a brief tussle with her younger brother about who had control of the big screen TV, but that was about it."

Trish pursed her lips thoughtfully. "I think that about does it then. Now I'd like to speak with your son, please."

"Sure, I'll get him," Ginny said.

As Ginny returned with her 9-year-old son in tow, the doorbell rang.

"Probably two of our officers who will be assisting me with the search," Trish explained.

Martin quickly got up from the sofa and opened the front door. Both officers Fricelli and Franks introduced themselves. "Where can we find Officer D'Amadeo, sir?" Franks asked. Martin pointed up toward the living room.

After quick introductions with Ginny, Trish asked Fric and Frac to canvas the neighborhood to see if anyone had seen the girl or anything suspicious during the night. Fric went up Rockridge Road while Frac hoofed it down to Ledgemere Drive. Ledgemere was right below and parallel to Rockridge. Both roads were part of a subdivision. Trish would question the neighbors immediately below the Gaines home.

Before interviewing the brother, Trish walked into the foyer and made a call to Chief Cook. "Chief, Trish here."

"What's going on there?"

"Chief, I think that this may be an abduction, maybe for ransom, hard to say. Doubt it is a runaway. The missing girl appears to be a well-adjusted, intelligent, well-liked youngster. Doesn't appear to be any family issues. Husband and wife appear to be loving, supportive, caring parents. No sign of spousal abuse, drug or alcohol addiction. So my best guess it is an abduction of some sort."

"OK, Trish. I'll be along shortly. I'll notify the state police and get the rest of our force out to canvass the school, local playgrounds and parks, just in case."

"Chief, I also strongly recommend we initiate an Amber Alert and register this incident with the National Crime Information Center."

"Agree. I'll do it now."

Trish returned to the living room, taking her seat across from the Gaines. The little boy, Marty Jr., sat between them. Unfortunately, the boy saw nothing, heard nothing and had no idea what had happened to his sister.

"It wasn't because we had the fight last night, was it?" He ventured with a worried expression.

"No, no," Trish reassured him as she patted him on the knee. "It had nothing to do with you, Marty, and thanks so much for answering my questions. You've been a big help," although he hadn't been and she didn't expect he would.

Trish stood up, nodded to the family and exited the house, heading down the hill to assist with the neighborhood search. She stopped momentarily at her police cruiser tossing Katie's laptop onto the passenger seat. As she began walking down the driveway she could taste the bile start to rise in her mouth.

5

There were three homes below the Gaines. The one immediately below on the left, bordering Katie's bedroom, was a very well maintained, white, front entrance colonial. A well-groomed lush border of holly, flaming bushes and box hedge flanked the entryway on both sides. In front on the left, there was a large Acacia dogwood that, in springtime, Trish mused, must be magnificent in full bloom. It stood in a carpet of thick pachysandra that spread out to a stonewall. A brick path led to the front entrance.

She was just preparing to knock on the door when it opened. "Good morning, officer," a balding man about 60, not much taller than Trish, stepped forward extending his hand.

"Hi, I'm Joe Capello. You here about Katie? You haven't found her yet?"

"No sir, we've only been here for about half an hour, but we're scouring the neighborhood now. Can you tell us the last time you saw her?"

"Sure," he began to answer, turning his head back into the doorway, nearly cracking his wife's skull with his own. "Christ, why'd you creep up on me like that?"

"Because I didn't know who was at the front door, nitwit," she said rolling her eyes with a look that told Trish what all women knew – all men were dolts.

"This is my wife, Lois," he said to Trish, then looked at his wife questioningly. "When was the last time we saw Katie?"

"I told the Gaines when they asked. It was yesterday afternoon, right after she was dropped off from the school bus. She stopped, like she usually does and played with the dogs for a few minutes, then went home," explained Lois, her face a blend of anxiety and concern. "I just hope you find that girl quickly. She is such a sweet girl," she said tugging her arms tightly around a worn bathrobe. "I would hate for anything to happen to her."

"That reminds me, officer." Joe interrupted anxiously. "Our dogs are missing."

"Your dogs are missing? When did that happen?"

"Well, it was around 4 AM."

"No Joe, it was more like 3:30," she corrected.

She nudged her husband in the side with her elbow. "Go ahead, tell her what happened. I'm here in case you forget any details, like what day it is."

"Some people you wouldn't mind see go missing," he said giving his wife a plaintive look. "So what happened? About 4 or make that…*3:30*, Shelly, our chocolate lab, starts to bark and this sets off Bosco, our bullmastiff. The dogs sleep in our bedroom. He gets out of his bed and jumps up on our bathroom window. So the missus here," he points to Lois, "naturally volunteers me to go downstairs and check out what the hell is going on to get the dogs so riled. So I throw on my bathrobe and slippers, go to the kitchen, grab a flashlight and look out the kitchen window over the sink to see if I can see anything. Da nada. Not a thing. Probably deer, I figure. Meanwhile, the dogs are right behind me still barking. So I go out the sliders to our back porch and open the screen door to take a better look out the back yard. I don't see anything but I did hear something from the direction of the woods leading up to the ridge in back of the house. Now I'm definitely thinking its deer. We get so many of them this time of year. They love dining on my hostas. Bastards!"

Trish raised her hand to have him pause a moment while she took notes. "Tell me, what kind of sound did you think you heard?"

"Well, deer running through underbrush. I've heard it many times before."

"So continue, please," Trish urged.

"I just turned around to go back into the house, when Bosco bounded past me into the yard with Shelly close behind. I called them back but when they're after deer it's impossible to stop them. They've done it before. Usually, they're back in an hour or so. Not this morning. Haven't come back yet."

"Is that unusual?"

"Yes, very," he said.

Trish closed her iPad, figuring she had learned as much as she was going to learn from the Capellos. "You've been a big help, Mr., Capello, Mrs. Capello. Would you be available later today if we needed to talk to you again?"

"Sure thing, anything we can do to help. And would you keep an eye out for our dogs."

"Will do, sir."

As Trish turned to leave, Lois gently grabbed the officer's forearm. "Please find her," Lois said with moistened eyes.

"We'll do everything possible to find her," Trish said, speaking with hope while thinking the unthinkable.

6

Once Lyle had identified the location of the target's home, he began his routine reconnaissance. The house was on a road that ran along the upper part of a ridge that extended about a half mile, terminating at Franklin Road. Franklin ran perpendicular to Ledgemere Drive that was below and parallel to Rockridge Road.

There were no homes above Rockridge. In fact, most back-yards on Rockridge were non-existent, comprising a steep, rocky grade that led to the top of the ridge. The ridge was bi-sected by a power company maintenance trail that ran below the power lines extending the length of the ridge.

Lyle did his cursory recon, ending on Franklin, where there was access to the maintenance trail. A padlocked, iron gate blocked the entrance. There was no fence on either side of the gate, so that access could be possible with an all terrain vehicle or a motorcycle. Lyle decided quickly that neither of those options was viable.

The maintenance road entrance, however, did provide space and cover for parking his SUV. It was flanked on both sides by large bushes. Someone had also dumped some construction debris to the right of the gate. There was a house diagonally across from the entrance but the sight lines were obscured.

Lyle exited the SUV, worked his way around the gate and began walking the maintenance trail. It was 1 AM. Off in the distance, he could see some shapes, most probably deer, he thought, making their way across the ridge. The baying of coywolves could also be heard. The sounds, together with the moonlight, chilled him.

There was a quarter moon, enough light to navigate by. He had to walk nearly the whole length of the ridge to come behind the target's house. He left the trail to the right. The ground was interspersed with small grasses and bushes. At the edge of the ridge, undergrowth and numerous aspens, oaks, maples and horse chestnuts obstructed the view of the homes below. From that point he could see the target's house slightly to the left, about 30 yards down the steep ridge face. He went through the trees, finding a rather crude path that ran down to a level area buttressed on the downhill side by a large stonewall. A series of stone steps were built into the wall to the right of the house, opposite the driveway.

From the rear, it appeared that all the bedrooms were on the ground level. He sat behind a stand of large rhododendrons, retrieving a pair of binoculars from his backpack. He stayed until morning, scanning each of the windows in the rear of the house. At about 6 AM the window shade in the extreme left of the house was pulled up. It was a woman in a bathrobe. She was talking to someone, when the target appeared. Yes!

The target slept in the left rear corner bedroom. It had two windows. The rear window faced the stonewall and was easily accessible from the ground. Access here should be no problem.

That night he turned on the local news for an update on the weather. In three days the skies would turn cloudy with a 60 percent chance of precip. Well, that sounded good enough. Best to work on a dark night. Thank god for moonless nights.

■ ■ ■

Even with all his careful planning, the abduction was still a close call. Initially, all went well. Lyle arrived at the trail maintenance gate at exactly 2:45 AM. He was completely clad in black clothing -- hiking boots, pants, sweatshirt, ski mask, and gloves. He also had a small, black backpack, a large hunting knife strapped to his left leg, a box cutter in his right hand pocket and a pair of night goggles strapped to his forehead. In the backpack he had a large zippered canvas bag and a small container with two vials of sedative and two syringes. Now, he thought, phase three – the abduction.

Lyle followed the exact route he had laid out during his recon. He arrived at the target's house at approximately 3 AM. He deftly made his way down to the window at the left rear of the house, careful to stay hidden in deep shadows. The night vision goggles, he grudgingly admitted, were worth every cent he had invested in them. He had bitched about the cost to his supplier but the bastard was right. They made it appear like it was daylight.

It was very quiet with only the sound of crickets and frogs from a nearby bog breaking the stillness. Crouched beneath the window, Lyle undid his backpack carefully, removing the canvas bag, the carrier belt and the syringe container. He took out the syringe, filled with the sedative, placing it in his left pants pocket. He then moved his backpack to the side, unfolding and unzipping the canvas bag that he spread out next to the window.

The first problem, perhaps a portent of things to come, was the window screen. It was either stuck or it had some interior latch. He fished out his box cutter, semper paratus, he thought smiling, and cut along the left and bottom seams of the screen. He pushed his arm through and began feeling along the screen frame. He found the latch at the bottom against the sill. Grabbing the screen frame from the outside, he slowly lifted it. It squeaked slightly, so he waited to see if it had aroused anyone. But all was quiet.

Lyle was surprised to see that the window was open about two or three inches. He slid the window up, being careful to do it slowly. Once up, he placed his hands on the sill and pushed himself up through the window. Countless hours at the gym were paying off handsomely.

The room was very dark but for the luminous dial on the nightstand clock. He pulled his night vision goggles back down over his eyes. Scanning the room he could see her bed against the right wall. She appeared sound asleep. He slowly walked up to the bed. Removing the syringe from his pocket, he leaned over her. His left hand moving quickly to cover her mouth.

Before she could react, Lyle had shoved the needle into her arm, pushing the 5 ccs of sedative into her body. He held her tightly, until he was sure the sedative had taken effect. Within twenty seconds she was unconscious, just as the supplier had promised.

From his left front pocket, he removed the belt. He wrapped it under her armpits, fastening it over her chest. He picked up her limp body and carried it to the open window. He put her legs through the window then, with *K's* admonition ringing in his head not to damage the package, he gently lowered her to the ground.

Slipping through the window, Lyle removed the belt from the target's chest. He picked her up and placed her in the middle of the open canvas bag. Out of his backpack, he grabbed a pair of plastic restraints, fastening one around her hands and the other around her feet. He covered her mouth with a piece of tape and zipped up the bag. To secure her body from slipping to the bottom of the bag, he tightly fastened the belt around her enclosed torso. He placed his right arm through one bag strap, then his left though the other. Leaning the left side of his body on the ground, he slowly rolled over to his right. With the bag on his back and his body on the ground, he brought first one knee, then the other up toward his stomach with his arms extended supporting his chest. He then brought his legs forward slowly standing up. He took a few steps re-adjusting the bag until he felt it was secure and comfortable.

Picking up his backpack, he folded it and put into his side pocket. The hardest part of his return trip would come now. With the package on his back, he had to negotiate first the stone steps, then the narrow, steep path to the top of the ridge.

He sucked in a breath and started toward the wall. The climb proved easier than he thought. He had a slight thigh burn but no pain, no gain. At the top of the ridge he checked his watch: 3:25. He had made excellent time. His self-congratulatory moment was quickly interrupted with the barking. Dogs! "What the fuck!" he mumbled under his breath.

Lyle hated dogs. Not because he had an intrinsic hatred for the species but rather because they were a major problem in his line of work. If the family of this girl on his back had had a dog, Lyle would never have gone near the house. They are just too unpredictable and loyal to a fault.

The barking was coming from somewhere farther down from the Gaines' home. Hopefully, the dogs were secured in a yard or a house. Meanwhile, they were waking the whole friggin' neighborhood. He began to move as quickly as he could, given the load he was carrying.

About half way down the ridge, Lyle was surprised to hear something or someone following behind him. He turned, his night vision goggles illuminating two green-lit bodies against one of the small hills that dotted the ridge. They were two dogs!

Now he pushed himself even harder. His breathing was labored and, though the night was cool, he was sweating profusely, as much from anxiety as from his exertions. Within minutes he could see the SUV beyond the gate. It was perhaps 50 yards away. He looked back one more time but he couldn't see the dogs, just hear them. No time, he had to hurry.

Reaching in his pocket he grabbed his car keys hitting the unlock button. He lifted the rear hatch while slipping the canvas bag off his back, slinging it unceremoniously into the rear of the vehicle. He slammed the rear door shut and made it into the driver's seat just as the dogs emerged from the side of the gate.

Lyle was just about to slam his door shut when jaws ripped into his wrist. He swallowed the scream the pain warranted, hearing his wrist bones and tendons snap under the pressure of the bullmastiff's jaws. Drawing blood, the dog released his hold, barking furiously, mounting the running board with his front legs.

Face to face, Lyle could only see the huge obsidian black pits of the dog's eyes and his enormous open mouth dripping globs of saliva. "Fuck!" he yelled slamming the dog in the chest with his left leg. The dog seemed oblivious, barking furiously. Pushing against the dog with his leg, he reached over with this good hand, grabbing his ankle knife. He thrust upward at the dog's broad chest but, sensing danger, the dog quickly jumped back, the blade tip barely catching flesh. Lyle saw his opportunity. Dropping the knife in the foot well, he grabbed the door handle with his good hand, pulling it closed.

Lyle was now drenched with sweat and experiencing what he hadn't experienced in a long time – fear. With his hands shaking, he fumbled for his keys in his right pocket. They weren't there. Don't panic, he told himself. Don't panic. He checked his other pockets, then the driver's side foot well. He began searching the other foot well, placing his hand on the passenger seat for support. The keys were there, under his hand.

The adrenaline still pumping, he quickly started the SUV, turning the steering wheel with his one good hand, as sharply as he could. It wasn't quite sharp enough as the vehicle went hurtling over the mass of construction debris that some local asshole had deposited on the side of the road. The dogs stood there barking at him as he accelerated on to the road. Keeping his lights out, he pulled his night goggles down. He would stay in this mode until he exited the neighborhood. Glancing back momentarily, he could see the dogs chasing him, the smaller of the two in the lead.

"Fuck 'em!" he said aloud, pressing down on the gas pedal.

7

Returning from the Capellos, Trish joined the command staff in front of the Gaines. They were busily organizing a more thorough search of the neighborhood.

"Trish, got anything," queried Chief Cook.

"Well, no one I talked to saw the girl. However, there was the curious incident of the Capellos' dogs."

"What's this 'curious incident' bullshit? Is this an Agatha Christie mystery?" The chief said irritatingly.

"No chief, more like Sir Arthur Conan Doyle. But it is *curious*," she responded, unperturbed by the chief's cutting tone.

"So tell us," Captain Fitzgerald interjected, diffusing the tension. "What about this 'curious incident'?"

Trish was just about to launch into her conversation with the Capellos when a black Chevy SUV pulled into the Gaines lower driveway. Definitely, she thought, a Feeb vehicle.

"Who's that?" asked Trish.

Fitzgerald turned to look. "Oh, must be the FBI's regional Child Abduction Rapid Deployment team, out of Boston. They specialize in missing children. The CARD team leader, Supervisory Special Agent Bill Ingram, is considered the best at what these teams do," the Captain explained.

"Who called them in?" Trish asked.

"They call themselves in. The CARD teams monitor all reports of missing children entered into the National Center for Missing and Exploited Children database. By law, the FBI has jurisdiction over all cases of missing children 12 and under, though they pick only those they believe requires their special know-how."

"And precisely what is their *special know-how*?" she asked rhetorically.

"Finding missing children," he said. "And they're very good at it."

Trish nodded as they all began to watch the Agents exit the SUV. The back seat passengers exited first. One was relatively short, but well built with tightly cropped hair. He was wearing a dark blue suit with appropriate accouterment, including a Glock, holstered on his right hip. The other was taller and leaner, also in dark blue worsted.

To save money, the FBI must buy these wardrobes wholesale, Trish mused. Certainly, neither had read, "Dress for Success." The driver then appeared. She was tall, perhaps a shade shorter than the agent who had sat behind her. She had broad shoulders with a lean, trim, and athletic body. A collegiate swimmer perhaps? She had long pale, blond hair coiffed neatly into a French braid. Though she had strong features, the square jaw, aquiline nose and Angelina Jolie lips combined to give her an exotic appearance. She was wearing a pair of black slacks tightly fitted around muscular legs and butt, a dark tailored blazer and a white form-fitting top.

She was very attractive, Trish admitted to herself. As a female police officer, Trish was always in competition with anyone and everyone, even when it came to other female officers.

The last to exit the vehicle, perhaps, a minute after everyone else was, Trish assumed, the team leader. He wasn't nearly what she expected. No blue suit, white shirt, dark tie, highly polished shoes. No, nothing like that. He appeared such an unpretentious sort of man. Almost like something out a Norman Rockwell painting except that this was 2014 not 1960!

Trish surveilled him from toe to crown. He was something else. He was taller than the shorter agent but shorter than either of the other two. Maybe, 5'9" or so. He wore practical, Timberland hiking boots, with heavy, light green cargo pants, a brown and green Harris Tweed jacket, leather lined on the pockets and elbows, a wool cardigan sweater vest, a blue checked button down shirt, and plaid bow tie. All gloriously topped off with a brown, felt Australian bush hat. All the clothes looked well worn.

Captain Fitzgerald waved to the Agents to join them. "Hi, Bing, sorry to see you again under these circumstances," he said as he shook hands with the retro-attired man in the tweed jacket.

"Good to see you Fitz. So whom do we have here?" he asked gesturing to the group.

The captain introduced the chief and Trish to Ingram. Trish took his hand firmly, always prepared with men, to be ready to exert as much hand pressure as possible. Guys liked to intimidate you that way. Crush your hand to mush just to prove a point. His grip was just firm enough. Good sign, she thought. He smiled too and it was a nice smile.

Ingram introduced the group to Special Agents Alexandra 'Ola' Dabrowski, Larry Coughlin and Leo Zito. The chief looked at Ingram. "Have you been briefed?"

"Yes chief. We spoke with your desk sergeant on the way here. Anything new since we talked?" Bing asked.

"Officer D'Amadeo was just updating us," Fitz said gesturing to Trish.

"Well, as I was telling the chief and Captain Fitzgerald, a pair of dogs are missing from a neighbor's home just down the road," she said, pointing to the bottom of Rockridge Drive. "What's *curious*," Trish glanced at the chief, "is that the dogs haven't returned. According to the Capellos, that is not like them. If they run off, they usually return within an hour or so, but this time they've been missing since about 3:30 this morning."

Ingram looked pensive. "About the time of the alleged abduction. Tell us exactly what happened with the dogs."

Trish opened her iPad and carefully reviewed her conversation with the Capellos. As she did, Ingram kept his right hand under his chin gently rubbing his lower lip back and forth.

"What are you thinking, sir?" Trish asked.

"Please Officer, call me Bing, everyone does," he said kindly. "I'm thinking that the *curious incident* of the missing dogs is more than 'curious'."

Trish cracked a smile, maybe too big of a smile. She noticed the chief cringe. "So, Supervisory Special Agent, I mean, Bing, what do you make of it?"

"First thing I'd do is put out a BOLO on the two dogs, with instructions not to approach them, but to identify and observe," Bing suggested.

"On the dogs," Fitz asked.

"Yah, on the dogs. I think they're tracking the girl. So we track them, a lot easier than tracking the girl. Incidentally, have you requested a K-9 unit?" he asked.

"Be here momentarily," said Fitz, a small smile crossing his lips knowing for once he was a step ahead of Bing, for now anyway.

"Why do you think it will be easier tracking the Capellos' dogs rather than the girl?" she asked Bing.

"The girl is probably being transported in a vehicle, lessening the availability of scent material, which already has had a few hours to degrade on the roadways" he explained patiently. "Also, the Capellos' dogs are leaving fresh scent of their own, most likely in areas that are relatively undisturbed. If they began following the trail almost immediately, and from what you've reported, that's exactly what happened, the dogs are staying relatively close, at least a helluva lot closer than we are."

"You're assuming that the dogs are trailing her and not after some deer or coywolf," she argued.

"Yes," he agreed, "I'm making that assumption based on what the Capellos have told you about their dogs. Sounds to me like Katie Gaines was their den mate. They appear to have an emotional attachment to her. If that's the case, they'll be far more effective finding Katie than our search-and-rescue dogs."

"Why's that?" Trish persisted.

"Because the two senses that canines have that are far superior to our own are those of smell and emotional intelligence," Bing said matter of factly. "Their emotional intelligence may even be keener than their sense of smell and that's about a million times more acute than our own."

"I still don't understand how their emotional intelligence can help them find Katie," responded a perplexed Trish.

"I'll explain, madam prosecutor, while you walk with me up to the Gaines' house so I can speak with them for a moment, and take a look at Katie's bedroom."

As they began walking up the driveway, Bing looked back at the chief, "Hope you don't mind me stealing her for a few minutes."

"No, not at all," replied the chief, "but remember you have to return what you borrow!"

8

As they walked up the driveway with the CARD team in tow, Trish turned to Bing. "So, Mr. Dog Whisperer, about the dogs," she said smiling.

"Have you ever had a dog, Officer?"

"Yes, when I was a kid."

"What was his name?"

"It was a she. We called her Bailey."

"Could Bailey read all your moods," asked Bing. "Could she tell when you were depressed or happy? Did anyone love you more than that dog?"

"I have to say yes to the first two and no to the third," replied Trish. "She was my closest friend. Bailey always knew what I was feeling."

"Well, then, that's emotional intelligence. But there is something more," ventured Bing. "Something that we can't quite explain. It is this inordinate attachment that dogs have for their masters. It defies explanation by any physical science because it is not explainable through any understanding of matter, time or space. Nevertheless, it is there and it is real."

"Yes," agreed Trish, "but can that emotional intelligence continue to guide them when they lose the scent?"

"Good question. But then, how can you explain that?" he said looking up at a flock of starlings engaged in their synchronized aerial acrobatics. "See that incredible display of synchrony. Looks like a wisp of black smoke tossing and turning."

"Biologists, mathematicians and computer specialists have all proposed explanations using algorithms and mathematical modeling. But it remains a mystery to us."

Trish looked up. "Point taken," said Trish, feeling like she had just lost an argument that she didn't think they were having.

"We should get up to the house," Bing said gesturing to his team to join them.

Bing walked ahead with Trish following. Ola caught up with her, bending close she whispered, "You've just had your first lesson from the professor. Feel blessed." Trish looked at a grinning Ola.

■ ■ ■

Bing was about to knock on the front door when it opened. A local cop stood there staring over Bing's shoulder at Trish. "Hi, Trish. Who do we have here," asked Officer Fracelli.

"This is FBI Supervisory Special Agent Ingram and his team," said Trish, "Special Agents Dabrowski, Zito, and Coughlin."

Fracelli nodded and gestured them in. "The Gaines are in the kitchen with one of the staties," said Fracelli. "Up the steps to the right."

The house was clean, well organized, and nicely decorated. Bing especially liked the large framed Audubon print of a loon hanging over the fireplace to the right of the living room. The main living floor was open, but cozy.

The Gaines, each with a cup of coffee held to their chests, their shoulders touching, were resting against a marble counter top, chatting with the Statie.

Trish walked ahead of Bing. "Mr. and Mrs. Gaines, the FBI is here and they'd like to talk to you briefly."

"The FBI!" said an alarmed Martin. "What are you doing here?"

Bing knew immediately what the father was thinking. *If the Feds are here, the local and state police must be baffled and very concerned. I need to reassure them.*

Bing approached the couple holding out his hand. "Hi, I'm SSA Bill Ingram. I know you must be thinking 'Why the FBI?' In cases like this," explained Bing, "the local and state police often call for our assistance to both consult and support. My team specializes in finding missing children, so we have quite a bit of experience and resources to share with local authorities. However, I can assure you that both the local and state police are doing everything they can to locate *Katie*."

The husband was about to say something when Ginny Gaines, staring directly at Bing, asked the dreaded question: "How many missing children are actually returned home ...

alive and well?" The *alive and well* spoken in a voice barely audible.

"That is a good question. Last year about a million children were reported missing. The vast majority were found within hours of being reported missing. And the vast majority of those," Bing emphasized, "are found *alive.*"

The Gaines seemed somewhat calmed by this information. Of course, Bing didn't give them all the statistics, since missing children fell into three broad categories and the stats for each differed. He knew that providing too much information was just a bad as too little and could be counterproductive. Among the data he held back was that, while deaths among missing children only occurred once in 10,000 cases, the statistics were much higher for 'stranger kidnappings' in which 20 percent of the missing children were found dead. And this case looked like a 'stranger kidnapping.'

When the intermittent silence told Bing that they had no more questions, at least for now, he asked permission to view Katie's bedroom.

"Of course," said Martin pointing to the corridor on their left.

Trish was impressed with how Bing handled the interchange with the Gaines. He had an avuncular, reassuring manner that was just what was needed. She could tell, however, he wasn't necessarily sharing all the stats about missing children. Then again, who would?

Trish led the way to Katie's bedroom. "Has the room been processed?" asked Bing.

"Yes, the staties finished about 30 minutes ago," said Trish.

"Good," he said while snapping on a pair of latex gloves.

Bing looked back at Ola. "Check on the Evidence Response Team. See when we should expect them." Ola dropped out of the group and immediately got on her cell.

As he entered Katie's bedroom Bing first went to the window that had apparently been used by the kidnapper. The other agents each took a part of the room and began systematically searching, for what, they didn't know.

"So this is what you reported to Chief Cook that made you suspicious about Katie's disappearance?" asked Bing pointing to the neat corner tear in the window screen.

"Yup, but that was the only thing that I could find. The room was just as you see it. Other than the messed up bedding, there was no sign of a struggle, no blood, nothing broken."

"So what made you suspicious that this just wasn't an adolescent prank?"

"From interviewing the parents, neighbors, friends and teachers, it appeared that Katie just wasn't that kind of kid. She was well behaved, a good student, loads of friends, and what appears to be two loving and involved parents."

An "Hmm," came from Bing as he began that continuous rubbing of his lower lip, while slowly surveilling the room.

"What are you thinking?" asked Trish.

"I'm thinking that this was a 'stranger kidnapping' but not your garden variety one," said Bing in a quiet, reflective voice.

"What do you mean?"

"Let's discuss this outside, shall we? Oh, one other thing, officer, Where is her laptop?

"How do you know she had a laptop?"

"De rigueur for youngsters these days. When we were kids our communication technology du jour was rudimentary — pad and pencil. Today, the ubiquitous laptop."

"Yes, I've got it in my cruiser," she said, thinking he must be a dad.

"Turn it over to Ola. She'll have our forensic people do the once over just in case this is the work of some online pedophile or an instance of cyber bullying."

"Will do."

As they were leaving, Bing turned to the Gaines. "Do you have a moment for a few questions?"

"Yes, certainly," Martin said pointing to the sofa in the living room. "Please have a seat."

Bing turned toward Ginny. "Mrs. Gaines, could I bother you for cup of tea?"

"What kind, Mr. Ingram?" She asked.

"Earl Grey or English Breakfast, if you have it."

Bing turned to face Martin. "Sir, what do you do for a living?"

"I'm a project manager for Raytheon. Anti-aircraft missile systems, mostly."

"Is that top secret, hush-hush kind of work?"

"Not really, just maintaining and upgrading current systems. Do you think that Katie gone missing has something to do with my work?" He sounded quite alarmed.

"No, no, sir. Just routine, we have to cover all the bases, all the possibilities." Bing nodded to Larry who was standing off to the left. He got on his cell immediately.

"How about Mrs. Gaines. Besides the full-time job of raising two, young children, does she have another job?"

"She's a middle school substitute teacher."

Ginny suddenly appeared between the two of them holding a teapot, three cups, a sugar bowl and cup of milk. "Milk and sugar, Agent Ingram?'

"Oh, I'll do that myself, thank you very much." He prepared his tea, brought the cup to his mouth and slowly sipped it with a somewhat exaggerated expression of pleasure. "Good, very good. Earl Grey. Love that citrus overtone of bergamot in the tea."

He smiled gently, looking at them both. "Can you tell me your combined financial worth?'

The Gaines looked at each other surprised and flummoxed by the question. "Haven't much thought about it, to tell you the truth," Martin said. "Hard to say. "Whadya think Ginny?"

"Well, let's see. We have about $150,000 equity in this house maybe close to $200,000 in both our savings and retirement plans. So not a helluva lot."

"More than most," Bing said. "More than most. And who is managing those funds for you or do you do it yourself?"

"No," Martin said. "My retirement plan is managed by Fidelity Financial Services and I also work with one of their financial advisors to manage our private portfolio, mostly mutual funds."

"I see." Bing nodded again toward Larry who was back on his cell.

Bing took one final large gulp of tea, wiping his lip with his finger. "Thank you so much, Mrs. Gaines, that was very refreshing. And thank you both for your cooperation."

As Bing stood up to leave, Ginny reached across the tray grabbing his arm forcefully. "Mr. Ingram, please – please get my baby back." Her eyes were welling up with tears.

Martin Gaines gently grabbed her from behind.

"Come Ginny, I'm sure the police are going to do every-thing in their power to find our little girl." He looked at Bing, his eyes as red as pomegranates. "Please, find her," he begged.

Bing leaned into the couple and whispered some thing that only they could hear. They nodded.

As they left, Trish turned to Bing, "What did you say to them?"

"Have faith," said Bing.

Faith in what or whom, she wondered.

9

Once Bosco and Shelly saw the shadowy figure moving through the tree line their barking became louder and more aggressive. They sensed Katie out there. Somewhere, not far. Their den mate was alone. Threatened. They could feel it, like waves coursing along a ship's bow.

Frank Capello stood on his deck piercing the darkness with the beam of his flashlight. He couldn't see a thing. *Enough of this*, he thought to himself. It was cold, so he hurried back into the porch, just not quick enough. He wasn't watching for his two dogs skulking near the porch door. As soon as he opened it, they were gone. By the time he turned around they were nearly across the yard.

Capello screamed for them to come back. But they weren't listening. They hardly ever did when it came to chasing deer. He spent the next 20 minutes looking for them while freezing his ass off. But no luck. He thought they'd return in an hour or two, which they usually did once the deer gave them the slip or they got bored.

■ ■ ■

Bosco and Shelly ran for the bushes behind the Gaines house. Immediately dropping their noses to the ground, swiveling them left, then right, up and down. Their nares flared as they inhaled copious amounts of microscopic material. Tens of thousands of molecules were being drawn into their bifurcated nasal passages. Particulate matter and bacteria were immediately trapped into the mucous layer that coats the passages. Molecules of scents and odors, however, were being drawn into a labyrinthine network of boney cartilaginous passages formed by the turbinate bones in the nasal cavity. These are lined with sensory cells populated with fine hair-like cilia that immediately began to analyze the chemical composition of each molecule trapped in the mucous layer surrounding them.

As each molecule was analyzed, the cells were sending the information to the olfactory bulb of each dog's brain. In fact, more than a third of their brains are devoted to this one function. That's the reason why a dog's sense of smell is more than a million times more acute than a human's.

The scent was identified immediately: heavy, oppressive, disturbing. Shared with the other parts of the dog's brain, those of emotion, memory and pleasure, an image arose. It was the dark hulk of the creature. Indistinct, fuzzy, but there. The dogs didn't associate the scent with an idea, a thought or a word. It appeared to them only as an image – an image of the creature. They began now to follow the scent in earnest.

They moved quickly up through the thicket of wild lilac and chokeberry, following the scent up to the tree line. Through the new growth of pine, oak and horse chestnut, they made their way into the open just below the power lines. The creature's scent took them to the maintenance path running parallel to the power lines. The area running below the power lines had been cleared of trees and bushes for about 50 yards in each direction.

Now they began moving quickly, as the scent grew stronger. Though the air was mixed with the odor of bushes, weeds, animal scat, and the decaying detritus of forested woodland, their noses kept them on course. Shelly had taken the lead, given her larger snout and more sensitive sense of smell. Her nares were flailing like butterfly wings opening then shutting as she exhaled, processing each smell with lightening speed.

They had gone no more than a hundred yards when they saw a shadow cresting a hillock up ahead. The creature's outline soon came into focus against the horizon dimly lit by the hazy glow from a street lamp. The dogs bounded into a quick trot, their noses continuously testing for scent.

Within seconds, they were on the crest of the hillock looking down at the street below. The creature was there, no more than 75 yards away. It had descended the ridge and was making its way around an iron gate. Bosco was the first to leap forward, his powerful leg muscles driving him down the hill. Shelly, slowed by arthritis, gamely followed, both barking madly.

10

As Lyle came to the crest of the hillock that overlooked where he had parked his SUV, he took a moment to catch his breath. He had been moving quickly. His constant hours of exercise and running were paying big dividends. He turned, his night goggles lighting up the path in an eerie green glow. There, about a hundred yards back, topping a small rise in the access road, were two animals – wolves, coyotes or dogs? Yes, they were dogs. Why would dogs be following him?

Lyle took another deep breath and looked back again. Now only about 50 yards and closing fast. Dammit, he thought. *They are chasing me.* He turned and descended the hillock quickly, dodging around the metal gate that barred vehicle access to the right of way.

He pressed a button on his key ring opening the SUV's rear door. Turning, he removed his left arm out of the strap flipping the back pack off his right shoulder into the vehicle's luggage compartment. As he pressed the button to close the rear door he could hear the dogs coming over the rise above the metal gate.

Lyle ran for the driver's door, pulled it open, hopping into the seat. He leaned over to close the door but an instant too late. The bullmastiff's enormous jaws tore into his forearm. The force of the bite tearing through skin, rupturing tendons and snapping his radius.

Hearing the bone crack, Lyle used all of his self-control to keep from screaming with pain. *Have to keep noise discipline.* That thought evaporated into the loud barking that came from the other dog, a manic chocolate lab.

Grimacing with pain, Lyle reached down with his one good hand to the knife strapped to his right ankle. He pulled it out and drove it straight for Bosco's chest. Seeing the blade flash toward him, the bullmastiff released his grip. With his front legs he sprung backwards as the tip of the blade ripped into his skin.

Because Lyle had to thrust across his body the knife barely penetrated the dog's chest, though enough to cause him to whelp with pain and retreat. With the dog backing off, Lyle dropped his knife into the foot well, grabbed the door handle and pulled it closed. He jammed the key into the ignition. He turned the front wheels as sharp as he could to avoid the pile of construction debris in front of him, jamming his foot down on the accelerator. There was a loud thud. The SUV bounced into the air then came down heavily with a crash, splintering wood and particleboard.

Luckily, no damage as the SUV skidded off the debris into the roadway. Lyle kept his foot on the accelerator. The vehicle quickly picked up speed. He looked into his rear view mirror. The dogs were running after him but gradually falling behind. With all the noise that attended his escape, he decided to drive with his lights off. He didn't want anyone to be able to describe the vehicle.

The adrenaline rush had yet to abate when Lyle turned the corner on to Last Mile Road. His turn was too wide. The SUV hit the shoulder of the road on the right, nearly hitting something. He veered sharply back onto the road. Looking into his side view mirror he saw nothing but heard a very load *"Asshole!"*

Lyle's first thought was to open the driver's side window and give the jerk the finger. But he couldn't feel his hand much less his fingers. *Who the fuck is out at this time of night?* He cradled his injured arm in his lap. The pain was growing slowly more intense as the narcotic effect of the adrenaline slowly dissipated from his body.

Now, finally, out of this pisshole of a town. Next step – deliver the package.

11

Bing and his team were gathered around the hood of the FBI SUV. He gestured to Fitz and Cook, who were talking to a group of police officers in the driveway, to join them.

Bing unrolled a large contour map of Wilton and its surrounding environs.

"Now we've been searching up here in this area," he said pointing to the contour lines of the ridge running above the Gaines home. "I'd suggest Chief Cook, your people and Fitzi's troopers continue searching with two of the search-and-rescue dogs along the ridge across this road here."

"That's Franklin Road," the chief explained. "How far do you want us to go?"

"To be safe, I'd go along the entire length of the ridge. That'll take you just beyond the town line," he said rubbing his lower lip intently. "Truth is, I don't think you'll find anything."

"Then why are we doing it?" the chief asked.

"We need to cover all the bases. Besides, I've been known to be wrong."

Bing looked over to Ola. "You've checked on sex offenders in the area?"

"Yes, boss," Ola responded, holding a laptop in her hand, "there are three. We've checked them all out. One guy is in the hospital suffering from an MI. The second is visiting his mom in Connecticut, been there all week. And the last guy, well, he had no alibi. Just said he was asleep at home."

"Could he be good for this?" Bing asked hopefully.

"Hardly. The guy is built like a bowling ball, short and weighing about three bills. He would have trouble getting off a toilet much less out of a window."

That brought grins from Fitz and the chief.

"Thanks, Ola," Bing nodded to her. "Where's Larry?"

"Right here sir," he said from directly behind Bing.

"Sorry, didn't see you there," he said chagrined. "I want you and Leo to work with Fitz's boys and start contacting everyone on the list of names we got from the Gaines. And I mean *everyone*."

"Gotcha boss, will do."

"Does anyone have anything to add?" asked Bing.

"Yah, I do," Larry piped up. "While I was in the house, the staties got a call from a guy by the name of Weston Pritchard who lives on Franklin. Says he was out jogging this morning around 3:30 when someone in a dark SUV nearly ran him over."

"Who the hell runs that early in the morning?" asked Bing.

"Exactly my question boss. He said he produces a sports talk program for a Boston station, so he has to be into work around five in the morning."

"Anything else."

"Yup. The guy that nearly hit him was driving with his lights off."

"That fits the time frame. Could be our perp. Let's get out another BOLO, this one on the SUV."

"Will do."

Bing was about to sum up what they knew and didn't know when Trish interrupted. "I don't understand why you think what we're doing now, the interviews and the search, aren't going to help us find Katie?"

"I think that it's evident that this is not a family member abduction or a pedophile abduction. Friends or acquaintances do not abduct children from their home in the middle of the night. It just doesn't happen. For the most part, abductions by pedophiles are almost always a crime of opportunity, a child left briefly alone or lost, becomes a target."

Bing now became very deliberate in carefully articulating his hypothesis of what might have happened.

"This is a stranger abduction but one performed by someone highly skilled who's done this before. He's a professional. This is what he does. I think Katie's disappearance is a case of stranger abduction for *hire*."

"For hire? What do you mean, Bing?" Fitzi asked.

"The perp was hired to find this girl, abduct and deliver her at a prescribed time and place," Bing said glancing at Fitzi.

The chief removed his cap and began scratching his head. "I just find this whole thing incredulous."

"You know Bing," Ola interjected," this could be…."

Shooting a withering look at Ola, Bing cut her off in mid sentence. "Ola, we going down this road again?"

"I'm just saying, boss, that this has all the earmarks of an Illuminati abduction."

Bing raised his hand to cut her off again when he thought better of it. "OK, Ola, why don't you share your thinking with the team," he said with an exasperated grimace.

"The Illuminati is a network of…"

Again Bing interrupted. "Alleged network, Ola… *alleged*!"

"OK, OK, have it your way. An *alleged* international network of very powerful and rich men who contract for the abduction of young girls and boys for the deviant practices of their member-ship," Ola spit out quickly to avoid another Bing interruption.

Before she could continue, Trish took her turn to interrupt. "Are these the same Illuminati that Dan Brown wrote about in 'The Da Vinci Code'?"

"Hardly, this group is as far from the one trying to pro-tect the descendants of Jesus Christ as Mother Theresa is from Hannibal Lecter."

"So why do you believe that they might be involved?" pur-sued Trish.

"It's the MO," she replied. "This is exactly what has been reported to be the standard practice of the Illuminati. Who else would kidnap a child from their home in the middle of the night, do it so expertly, after spending considerable time sur-veilling the child?"

"How do you know they spent time surveilling?" the chief asked with a quizzical look.

From the back, Leo pushed by Ola whispering to her as he moved by, "I've got your back on *this*."

"It's obvious, chief," Leo argued, "that the perp knew the child's daily routine, where she resided in the house, when she went to bed, where to enter the house, how to egress and what escape route to use. This was a well-planned abduction, all signs of the, um.....*alleged* Illuminati network."

"So Bing, what do you have to say for yourself?" an amused Trish asked smiling.

Bing frowned at Trish. "Remind me never to give the floor to those two again."

He took a deep breath. "To answer your question, I believe that, as Ola theorizes, this could very well be the work of some sort of network that does abductions for hire. Their MO is consistent with that reported for the Illuminati. But there is no concrete proof that the Illuminati exists other than fanciful reports on the Internet. Neither Interpol nor any national police organization has ever reported on an abduction with an Illuminati connection. It's a great conspiracy theory worthy of another Dan Brown novel. But like most conspiracy theories it is complex, fanciful and entirely without proof."

"Now, let's focus on what we do know and not waste time on the improbable." Bing looked at his wristwatch. "Everyone has their assignments, so I suggest we get the hell moving. Time is running short …"

12

Katie was cold.

She had had the scariest nightmare.

Must wake up from it.

She opened her eyes. But she couldn't see.

She tried to speak. But her mouth wouldn't open.

She couldn't move her hands or legs.

Was she still dreaming? What was happening to her?

She needed to wake up. She wanted so desperately to scream, but all she could manage was coughing up foul tasting bile into her mouth.

No, this wasn't a dream. This was happening to her.

She panicked.

Katie began to pull against the plastic restraints on her hands and feet. She swung her body fiercely from side to side. She smashed her head against the bag repeatedly. Finally, having dug the restraints into her now bloody wrists and ankles, and rubbed her forehead raw, she relented.

She began to cry. Exerting all of her self-control, she managed to stifle the sound of her crying, but not the tears. They rolled down her face, as her body shivered with fear and anxiety.

Calm down Katie, she said to herself. *Remember what Daddy always said to you whenever you felt afraid. 'Fear paralyzes action. Action paralyzes fear.' Now, you must take control of your fear by taking action. You need to be smart Katie, think about what you can do to help yourself. What can you do?*

She thought about the time her father had talked to her about dealing with Maxie Dolman, the 'enfant terrible' of middle school. Maxie was big for her age, five foot eight and she must have weighed 170 lbs. and muscular for a girl. Maxie didn't much like anyone, including herself. She terrorized every girl in the school and most of the boys. Unfortunately, Katie was one of her favorite targets. Kalinda, Katie's best friend, told her that Maxie hated Katie because she was everything that Maxie wasn't – nice, friendly, well liked, smart and pretty, very pretty. So as long at they were in middle school, Kalinda warned, Katie was going to have to deal with Maxie Dolman.

As usual, her dad gave her sound advice. Use humor to deflect her comments and insults. Let her know that they don't bother you. Eventually, she'll tire of you and pick an easier mark. But, he said, and this is a big BUT, if she ever lays a hand on you then it's all out war! Because she's too big to go mano y mano, use anything at hand and hit her as hard as you can. She'll get the message. And remember, I'll always have your back.

Instinctively, Katie knew not to share this most recent piece of advice from dad with mom because, well, mom was non-violent, except when it came to her father. Not much later, Maxie caught up with Katie standing in line for her school bus.

"Hey prissy Katie," the words dripping slowly from Maxie's lips. "I hear that you like to take it in your mouth."

Katie turned and with a straight face retorted, "I thought that you had a monopoly on that practice!"

Everyone laughed and Maxie went into a rage, swinging wildly at Katie. She ducked, Maxie's fist just grazing the top of her head. Katie reached across her body with her right arm, grabbing her backpack from off her shoulder and swung it as hard as she could in a wide arc, hopeful that this would at least move Maxie from getting too close to her. But instead of air, Katie felt a heavy thud and then heard Maxie screaming.

Katie, adrenaline rushing through her body, turned around to see Maxie laying on the ground, a trickle of blood rolling down from her nose to her chin. Katie was terrified of what Maxie would do once she got up. But Maxie didn't get up. She just lay there crying and swearing at no one in particular.

That altercation led to her first and only parent-principal conference, a week's detention for both girls, and Katie's grounding for a month. As they left the principal's office, Dad put his arm around Katie's shoulder.

"Katie, I said it was OK to defend yourself but not necessarily with the whole Library of Congress that you carry in that backpack. Though I must admit, it was effective!" He grinned, squeezing her shoulder approvingly. Her mother could do nothing but roll her eyes at the two of them.

Maxie Dolman never bothered Katie again. As a matter of fact, she never bothered anyone else again. The following year she moved with her family to Connecticut.

So be ready to do what you have to do when the time is right. But first things first. How am I bound? Feels like plastic bands on my hands and feet. They're tight. No getting out of these, regardless of how hard I struggle. Something else around my waist, like a belt. Also very tight. Without my hands free I can't do much about that. What about what I'm in? Some sort of large canvas or nylon bag? Tough material, with a zipper maybe? But I can't feel one.

Now, where am I? I can feel movement, up and down jostling. Definitely some vehicle. Can hear the hum of the engine and the tires move across the road with an occasional bump or two. It's not a car. Too spacious. An SUV maybe? Having rolled in the bag against the sides of the vehicle, she knew it is the width of nearly one complete roll. Very roomy interior. Yes, an SUV!

Bound this way there's not much I can do. Eventually, they'll have to take me out of the bag, maybe even cut the nylon bands. Then what should I do? Remember that Lifetime movie you saw with mom about the girl kidnapped? You asked mom why the girl was being so submissive, doing exactly what she was told, never putting up a fight. You couldn't understand her behavior. Your mother said that's because I think she's playing possum.

Playing possum? Yah, your mother explained. She wants them to think that she's too frightened to resist and that she'll do anything they want her to do so that they won't harm her. But wait, as soon as their guard is down, she'll run. Just you wait.

Mom was right. She was playing possum and it worked.

That's what I'm going to do – play possum. Then I'll run and I won't stop running!

So what have I learned? I'm bound hand and foot, secured in a canvas or nylon bag being transported in a roomy SUV. But why? Why me? For, ransom? Mom and dad don't have much money. This is so crazy! Why have they done this?

And who is "they"?

13

Lyle was finally beginning to relax, having finally made it out of Wilton. However, he eschewed heading for the highway. He wanted to keep as low a profile as possible so he'd stick to the secondary roads until rush hour when he could more easily blend in with the traffic.

Once out of Wilton, he began searching for a quiet spot to park for a moment. He had to tie up his left arm. Hanging the arm loose only served to exacerbate the pain and it was painful. He found a clearing on the side of the road, running north toward Rte. 2. The vegetation had been pushed back from the road allowing for a 15-foot space between the road and the woods that bordered it.

When he stopped, he removed his belt. He slid it around his neck, locked it with the buckle, gingerly placing his arm in the makeshift sling. Wasn't perfect but it would have to do. He was quickly back on the road.

That brief moment of relief he was starting to experience after his escape from Wilton soon disappeared. He began to feel the SUV pulling to the right and his steering felt compromised. There was also a strange thumping sound from the front of the vehicle. He knew from experience that this was not good.

Once again, he began searching for a spot that he could pull into without being noticed. Another 10 minutes of driving took him to a small dirt road that led into the woods for some 50 yards of so. Good enough.

Lyle got out of the vehicle and walked apprehensively to the front inspecting first the left and then the right wheel. Dammit! It was the right wheel, nearly flat. He examined it carefully, feeling along the threads with his fingers. He saw and felt the nail at the same moment. It was fully embedded into the tire just above where the tire met the dirt road.

Where the hell did that come… from the pile of construction debris I ran over in Wilton? Great. Just great. What a clusterfuck this has turned out to be!

Fingering his painful left arm, Lyle knew that trying to change the large SUV tire with one good arm would be an exercise in futility. However, while he had been on the road for more than an hour now, there was still some air left in the tire. These tires were made to self-repair at least for a time. Naturally, he couldn't make it to the original rendezvous point with K. But maybe the alternate would work.

He retrieved his cell phone and called K.

"Lyle," K answered with a hint of distress. "What's the matter?"

"A bit of a problem. Need to change plans," he said trying to convey a sense of normalcy. "I won't be able to get to the prearranged rendezvous as planned."

"What the hell happened?"

"It's a long story. Tell you when we meet. Let's meet at my cabin outside of Royalston. How long will it take you to get there?"

For a few seconds there was silence on the end of the line. "Dammit, Lyle! How the hell did you screw this up? We've got a quarter of a mil on the line here. Jeez!"

"Calm down. Remember, *K*, I'm the one taking all the chances. You just sit there at home waiting for me to do all the heavy lifting. So cut the fuckin' complainin' and tell me how long it will take you to get to the cabin, for crissake!"

"You're an asshole!" *K* spit out. "I'll be there in about an hour and a half."

"Just get there as soon as possible and don't fuck around!" Lyle hissed and then hung up.

Calling me an asshole. What a fuck. Lazy prick!

14

A few miles outside of Wilton, Bosco and Shelly were having problems picking up the scent. They had left the woods that paralleled the road and were slowly making their way along the road that Lyle had taken. The scent was thin and then disappeared altogether, for a time.

They knew, however, that he had been here with their den mate. They were feeling the ripples that flowed through their consciousness. The unmistakable fluctuations of senses finely attuned to a member of their pack.

Humans could not understand or even begin to fathom the nature of a dog's consciousness. While humans assume that they have consciousness they deny its existence in other carbon-based life forms. They consider their consciousness far superior, reflected in the Jungian declaration that "I think, therefore I am." Dogs, however, are instinctual, not conscious thinkers, like humans, they argue.

But what humans do not know is that dogs not only have a consciousness but one that in many ways is far superior to that of humans. For human consciousness is all about the "I". Not so with the world of dogs. No, dogs do not think in terms of "I".

A dog does not consciously argue: "I think therefore I am," but rather knows that "I sense therefore we are." It is a consciousness of the pack. When a pack member is missing, it causes a disturbance in their consciousness that is as sensitive as sonar. And that sonar was giving off signals now.

As Bosco looked up from the roadbed, he saw Shelly focusing intently with her nose at a spot a few feet from the side of the road. He trotted over putting his thick, wet, fleshy nose next to hers, getting a snoot full. That was it – the scent. They had found it once again.

Shelly picked up her nose and tilted it into the air, sniffing voraciously. She dropped her nose to the road once again and began tracing a path toward the clearing at the side of the road. She stopped briefly, taking one last good snoot full before bounding off along the road.

Too preoccupied with the scent that Shelly had found, Bosco was busy working his nose over the roadbed and hadn't noticed the lab's quick departure. When he raised his head to look for her all he could see was her chocolate tail waving rapidly side to side some 50 yards further down the road. The bullmastiff quickly launched himself, sprinting after her.

For the dogs, the scent was strong, their symbiotic consciousness raised. The hunt was on.

15

Bing, Ola and Leo had joined with the local and state police in their search of the ridge behind the Gaines home. Some 20 police officers were involved, spread out in a line 100 yards across the ridge, moving north toward Franklin Street. A two-dog, State K-9 unit was leading the procession. They were German Shepherds named Tom and Giselle.

The dogs were making good progress. At Bing's urging, they had been given bedding from the Capello's dogs. After a moment of sniffing, they had set out quickly, their noses easily following Bosco's and Shelly's scents. They finished searching the ridge in half an hour.

As they descended the ridge they passed by the iron gate. The dogs stopped here moving in concentric circles, their ears standing straight up, along with the hair running down the ridge of their backs. They were excited.

Bing watched them. "Seems like they were here, that's for sure."

But then the dogs began tacking off to the right, following Franklin Road away from the ridge.

Trish turned to Bing. "One of our officers talked to the guy who lives over there," she said pointing to a house further down Franklin and across the street. "He said he had heard some noise and what he thought were dogs barking around 4 AM or so. Could be our guy."

"Consistent with what the jogger reported," Bing said his eyes tracking Tom and Giselle as they headed down Franklin.

Bing gestured to Fitzi and the Chief. "Let's split up. You take your officers and finish combing the ridge north of here, just in case. Meanwhile, my team and Officer D'Amadeo, we'll follow the K-9 unit, see where they lead us."

"Sounds like a plan," Fitzi said.

Fitzi, the Chief and the state and local officers crossed the road, continuing their search of the ridge. Bing waved to them as his group trotted to catch up to the K-9 unit that appeared to be moving quickly along Franklin.

"If he's got a vehicle, we'll never catch him on foot," bemoaned Ola.

"You're right, but at least we'll have a vague idea of what direction he's headed," Bing admitted. "Besides, we have nothing to do right now except to hope that our BOLOs get a response, then maybe we can jump ahead a bit and catch up to the UNSUB."

"Do you think we'll get a hit?" Trish asked.

"I'll bet on it," he answered emphatically. "Two dogs, very recognizable breeds, traveling on their own. They'll be spotted. Hopefully, sooner rather than later."

16

When Lyle had checked out the front tire he could see that he didn't have much time before it would go completely flat. The large nail embedded in the tread was slowly leaking out air. He had to find a service station with an air pump. Finding one on these side roads would be difficult so he cut over to a state road that continued north.

The state road was busier with more of a chance that he could be spotted if they had a BOLO out for his SUV, but that couldn't be helped. He needed air.

Within 10 minutes he spotted a Mobil station with a convenience store. He drove up to the front searching one side then the other for an external air pump. No luck!

It was amazing, he thought, how many of these stations didn't have air pumps. Cheap sons-of-bitches or was it that the newer tires were so much more reliable? When he caught himself thinking these random thoughts, he shook his head back and forth as if the shaking would clear his mind. He needed to concentrate, to stay in the moment.

Another 15 minutes, another station with no air pump. Problem with living in this part of the state, people here think it is the end of the world – air not needed!

Lyle continued on the road, driving carefully and within the speed limit. One good thing, the girl was quiet. No more crying. Not a peep since about an hour ago.

Finally, he spotted another service station, this one also with a small coffee shop and repair bays. They should have air. As he drove up toward the gas pumps, he could see an air pump on the far side of the building. He pulled over with his front right tire as close to the pump as possible. He grabbed his pressure gauge from the glove compartment, exited the SUV and casually strolled to the air pump, carefully looking around to make sure no one was watching.

The pump costs 50 cents. *A half-buck for air. Christ, we breathe it for free and they're charging for it. Capitalism gone wacko!* Random thoughts again.

A disgruntled Lyle checked the tire's air pressure; it was less than 10 PSI, damn near flat. He filled it to the required 32 PSI. Hopefully, he'd make it to the cabin before he'd need to find another air pump.

When he rewound the pump hose he carefully peered around the corner of the building to insure that no one was there. He pulled back quickly as a BMW pulled up and parked to the side of the building. The driver, a tall, trim and attractive woman maybe in her late thirties with fuck-me spiked heels, exited. She entered the convenience store, probably to pick up a caffeine pick-me-up on her way to work.

If I wasn't on a job, he thought, I'd gladly give her a pick-me-up.

With the coast temporarily cleared, he got back in the SUV, exiting on to the road quickly, heading north. He estimated 45 minutes to the cabin.

Lyle retrieved his cell phone from his pocket and dialed *K*.

"Lyle, do you have more good news to report." The words sounding more sarcastic than he wanted.

Deciding that getting into a verbal pissing match with this pissant wasn't the right call just now, Lyle kept his cool.

"Just a friendly call to let you know that I should be arriving at the cabin in about 30 minutes. See you there," he said sharply.

"Good," *K* said flatly.

Lyle followed Route 2A, crossing under State Highway 2, to Route 202 toward Baldwinville. Half way to Baldwinville he turned off 202 going northwest toward South Royalston. Just after passing through that small burg he exited onto a small dirt road.

Up ahead, through the woods, he could finally see the cabin. Now to unload his package and make her asshole *K's* problem. His job was done.

17

Falling into an easy canter, Bosco and Shelly moved along the edge of the state road. Their noses either stuck perpetually to the roadway or up in the air. They were both dragging in copious amounts of air. Analyzing tens of thousands of molecules of roadway detritus. On occasion catching that one elusive molecule that would tell them they were on the right track.

There it was again.

A microscopic piece of human runoff.

Perhaps, a cell from skin, hair or mucous, undeniably the creature's.

Each molecule setting off instant flashes in the dogs' brains. Pictures of the man, like snapshots in a camera, one after the other – the man who had Katie.

A cool breeze started to blow in the dogs' faces. Refreshing but also telling. It carried new data – new scents, odors. Stronger now.

Yes, it was the man, further on, but not far. Keep going. They were getting closer and closer. So close they could sense it and her – the den mate.

The scent now was almost unmistakable and omnipresent. It came from a building on the side of the road. Cars were parked in front and to the side. Some stood in a line, waiting.

This was the place. They had been here. And recently.

The dogs ran into the service station's lot, dodging among the vehicles, sniffing wildly for that one sign that they had been here. There was nothing on the right side of the building or on the front. But, then, on the left, near this thing that lay curled up and hung on the wall. Yes, here, it had been. The scent unmistakable and recent.

Shelly became very excited and agitated simultaneously. Looking first left, then right, searching for something. Then she had it. To the right, to the right, up the road, that's where it had gone.

The dogs moved out of the service station lot onto the shoulder of the road. They began to move in a slow trot then they ratcheted up to a canter. The scent was stronger and so was the feeling that rippled through their consciousness. It was ahead. She was ahead.

They began to run.

18

They had been following Tom and Giselle for 45 minutes, well beyond the Wilton town limits. The road they were on was leading them north by northwest. While making progress, Bing knew that they needed a break and they needed it soon if they were to rescue Katie. Too much time was passing.

Bing's thoughts echoed those of Ola. He looked back at her with a hopeful smile. "Don't worry, Ola, it's coming."

"What's coming?"

"That piece of good luck we're hoping for."

"Hope so. We need some."

Trish looked at Ola. "I've got a feeling we're going to get the bastard."

"I just hope that we find the girl," Ola replied anxiously. "This is too damn slow going."

Pachelbel's Canon started to fill the air. "What's that?" Trish asked startled.

"Just my cell," Bing said.

"Bing here. Yah…. great news, thanks." Bing shut the phone off and turned smiling to the group. We've got a hit on our BOLO. A local cop in Templeton spotted the dogs at a service station."

Bing yelled to the K-9 unit staties. "Get Tom and Giselle into the van. We're heading north."

He turned to Ola. Get the SUV. We've got a lot of ground to cover.

A few minutes later the caravan was headed north with sirens blaring.

19

Ola was a mad woman. She was turning in and out of traffic while plowing ahead at 90 miles an hour.

"Ola! We've got to get this guy but we need to be alive to do it," Bing said between gritted teeth.

"Bing, have I ever had an accident? No! Never! And I'm not going to start now. Squeeze your legs tight and stop pissing your pants."

As Ola swerved from the middle into the passing lane, just missing the rear of a truck, Bing nearly lost it. "Ola! Dammit. One more move like that and you'll have my bagel and egg breakfast in your lap."

"Men," Ola said glancing back to an ashen-faced Trish. "I can't understand how they can rule the world."

"Probably because they don't drive like they have a death wish," Trish just managed to spit out.

Ola looked up to catch Leo in the rear view mirror. "Now, Leo, am I going too fast?"

Leo's eyes flickered open. "What?"

"Nothing Leo. Go back to sleep. See, my driving is actually quite soothing."

Trish looked over at Leo. "I think it is more like he had a near death experience."

"Well, not to worry," a defiant Ola said. "We're almost there."

The black FBI SUV came to a screeching halt in front of the service station. A local police cruiser was parked next to the building with a police officer leaning against it.

"Dis must be da place," said a smiling Ola.

Ola bounced out of the vehicle while the others moved more hesitantly. Leo, because he was groggy from sleep and Trish and Bing because they were grateful to be alive. A minute later, the Mass State Police van with the K-9 unit pulled in behind them.

The local cop walked over to Bing and introduced himself. "Officer O'Callaghan. I'm the one who responded to the BOLO."

"SSA Bing Ingram," Bing said shaking the officer's hand. "Can you tell us exactly where you saw the dogs and what they were doing?"

"Well, I had pulled into the station to get a cup of coffee when I saw first one, then another dog appear from between two parked cars to the right of the service station. They were sniffing the cars up and down," he explained.

"Now sometimes you get strays in the area but these were two good looking dogs. I didn't know what type the big guy was but the chocolate lab was unmistakable. That's when I made my call. Last time I spied the dogs they were heading that way," he said pointing to the woods to the left of the service station.

Gesturing toward the road adjacent to the woods, Bing asked, "Where does that road go?"

"Parallels Route 2 then heads up toward South Royalston, not far from the New Hampshire border," the patrolman said.

"Thanks," Bing said. "Appreciate your help."

Bing gestured to the K-9 unit State Troopers pointing to the woods. "Get Tom and Giselle and start them in those woods over there. We'll follow."

"Leo," Bing called turning his head around. "Where the hell is Leo?"

"I'm right behind you boss," a deadpanned Leo responded.

"Could you please do me a favor and stay where I can see you," Bing said pleadingly. "You take the vehicle and follow. Give a call to Larry to inform the rest of the group where we are and what we're doing and have them join us ASAP. Capisc'?"

"Mia piace quando parli Italiano, capo," Leo chuckled as he moved off toward the FBI SUV with his cell already to his ear.

Ola yelled at Leo as he walked away. "What the hell did you say?"

" 'I love it when you speak Italian, boss,' " he yelled back.

Bing shook his head, looking over at Leo. "Now if you can only learn English!"

Bing turned to Ola and Trish. "We best get going and follow the dogs before the trail gets cold." The two women fell in behind Bing, heading off into the woods.

■ ■ ■

Less than 50 yards into the woods Tom and Giselle began tacking off back toward the road. They exited the woods down a slight culvert and onto the shoulder of the one-lane state road, still heading north. They began almost instantly picking up the pace.

The team began making their way down the road as traffic began piling up behind the two FBI vehicles. They were slowly trailing the entourage though hugging the shoulder as tightly as they could while avoiding skidding into the culvert that bordered the road.

Noticing the traffic pileup, Bing asked Ola to get on her cell to the local PD. "Request that they send a couple of officers down here to move the traffic around us."

Ola nodded and dropped back from the group momentarily while she called on her cell.

Trish took the opportunity to walk beside Bing. "This a typical case for your CARD team?" she asked in an effort to make conversation.

"Nothing is typical in this business, officer. But I will admit that this is somewhat unusual. Never had the assistance of neighborhood dogs in tracking down an UNSUB."

"Please, call me Trish. 'Officer' sounds rather officious."

"Sorry, didn't mean to offend, *Trish.* Is that short for Patricia?"

"No actually, I was christened Trisha. My aunt's idea."

"Well it fits you."

"How so?" She inquired smiling.

"Just the way that Tom and Giselle fit those two search dogs," he smiled back.

"Never been compared to a dog, but they are cute."

You are too, Bing thought but didn't say it. Have to remain professional. He let out a low laugh, as he picked up the pace to keep up with the two search dogs.

Trish dropped back, joining Ola. "He likes you," Ola said. "Give him time, he'll warm up."

"Should I care?" Trish asked.

"I don't know. Should you?" She stared at Trish for a moment. "You look interested to me."

Trish blushed. "Shows, huh?"

"Hey, he's a good guy. They're hard to find. I can relate."

"How about you," Trish asked. "Ever have any interest?"

"Yah, but I soon realized that we would be friends and colleagues, and nothing more, though I'm grateful for that. A relationship just would have mucked things up. Besides, I was a bit interested but he never was. He still missed his wife."

"How about now?" Trish asked hopefully.

"I think he's ready. It's been awhile, besides," Ola ventured, "you're the first woman that he's ever showed any interest in. I mean *real* interest."

Trish blushed again. She felt like a teenager interested in her first beau. Foolish to be thinking about a man in the middle of all this. But she couldn't help herself, she liked him. She suddenly had to refocus when a tree branch slapped across her face.

Bing looked back at her, "Sorry about that. Didn't realize you were so close behind."

"My fault," Trish confessed. "I should know better than walk behind a man!"

About a half hour later a Massachusetts State Police SUV with blue and red lights blinking came up the road behind them. It was Fitzi and Chief Cook with two State SWAT team members in the rear.

Bing waved. "Nice of you to join us."

"We'll follow in behind the caravan," Fitzi said. "How're we doing?"

Bing stopped for a moment. He removed his Barmah Australian bush hat and wiped his brow. "Slow going, but the dogs have the scent. Let's hope we chase this guy to ground soon."

■ ■ ■

Tom and Giselle kept mostly to the side of the road, dodging into the bushes and woods occasionally, but always returning to the roadway. An hour later, they suddenly stopped. Both put their snouts to the ground, working it meticulously. They were processing copious amounts of scents but Bosco and Shelly's now eluded them. So they back tracked.

Bing, Ola and Trish stood there watching Tom and Giselle do their thing. Tom started moving back down the road the way they had come with Giselle following. Both stopped, leaving the road into a small clearing in the woods that bordered the road. They stood sniffing, and then began pulling their handlers through the low bushes onto a narrow dirt road with worn tire ruts divided by a mound of over grown weed and grasses. The road wound its way into the thick woods disappearing as it curved slightly to the left.

Bing jogged over to the dog handlers. "Hold here for a moment."

Turning to Ola and Trish he gestured for them to join him. "I think that this is where we're going to find him."

Bing walked back to talk with Fitzi and the Chief in the SUV. Fitzi rolled his window down. "What's up?"

"I think he's hold up down this dirt road here," he said pointing to where Ola and Trish stood.

"Here's what we'll do. I'll go with Ola, Leo and Officer D'Amadeo along with the K-9s up the road to see what we find. Meanwhile, let's block off this roadway just in case. And give the locals a call to let them know what we're doing here and to ask for assistance with traffic control."

Bing walked over to the FBI SUV, waving to the others to join him. Leo let the passenger side window down. "What's the plan, boss?"

"We're doing a little recon. Get your vest on."

Bing went to the rear of the SUV, retrieving his protective vest emblazoned with the FBI imprint on front and back. He grabbed two others, tossing one to Ola and the other to a surprised Trish who made a nice recovery grabbing it out of the air with her left hand.

"Expecting trouble," Trish asked.

"Always."

The group walked over to where the K-9 unit stood. "Everyone check your weapons." The dog handlers were busy putting protective vests on Tom and Giselle.

There followed the sound of weapons unholstered, magazines checked and safeties unlocked.

Just as Bing was ready to say "Let's go," a white van appeared around the bend in the dirt road and then stopped.

A surprised Bing looked at the van.

"The plot thickens!" he murmured.

20

Katie had been lying quietly in the back of the SUV. Since Lyle's brief conversation with the mysterious *K* sometime ago, he had been silent. They had stopped briefly somewhere for about 5 minutes then on the road again. A smooth ride until a few minutes ago. The vehicle had nearly stopped, slowly taken a sharp right turn, then a very bumpy ride for a quarter of a mile or so.

When they came to a stop, she heard the driver side door open, then the rear door. "We're here, finally. Let's get you up."

Grabbing her ankles through the canvas bag, he dragged her to the edge of the luggage bed. He unzipped the bag.

Katie squinted. The light was blinding.

Lyle pulled the bag off her legs. "I'm going to cut the restraints on your feet. If you try to run I'll catch you and then I will hurt you, very badly," he warned in a voice that was threatening in its calmness.

Katie nodded. *Playing possum!*

"Good girl." Lyle took his pocketknife and cut the plastic restraints on her feet. He stood her up and gave her a moment to get her sea legs. He turned her toward the cabin and pushed her forward.

Katie stumbled but quickly regained her balance. Be submissive; show compliance, she reminded herself. She began to walk as steady as she could in the direction that Lyle was pushing her.

Playing possum!

The cabin was small. It had a slight overhang, supported by two posts, and anchored to a wooden deck that was only about 8 inches off the ground. Two windows, one on each side, flanking a door in the front. One window on the left side of the house. The house was slightly angled to the right so only the left side was visible from the road. The clapboard siding had been painted white sometime in the Lincoln administration. Every board appeared to be peeling. A chimney protruded above the roof peak on the right side of the building.

"Hi Mom, I'm home," said a chuckling Lyle as he unlocked the door. He took Katie's arm and led her to a chair next to a table that stood to the right of an old rectangular wood stove.

"Now you sit here and be a good girl while I get us something to eat."

Katie nodded, watching Lyle intently, but averting her eyes whenever he looked at her. She started to think about escaping. The door was only about 10 feet from where she sat, but with her hands still restrained, it would be nearly impossible for her to open it and get out before he could grab her. Must wait. Try to get him to cut her wrist restraints.

Play possum.

Lyle began rummaging through a cabinet over a rust stained sink. Retrieving a can of Dinty Moore's beef stew, he examined it carefully.

"Well, well, lookee here. Only a year old. Should make a passable repast."

He took a seat next to Katie. With his pocketknife he opened the can. From a small draw under the table he withdrew a plastic spoon. "Only the best silverware," he chortled pointing it toward Katie.

He took a couple of spoonfuls, slowly masticating the flour thickened mass. "Excuse my manners young lady, I should remove that," as he quickly ripped the tape off Katie's mouth.

"Sorry if that hurt but it's always better to do it quickly. So how about a little nourishment, huh?" he asked pushing a hefty spoonful of stew toward her mouth.

Katie took the stew and began to chew, a grimace crossing her face.

"What's the matter, no like? Huh?"

Lyle took another huge mouthful, chewing and swallowing the stew, while allowing some to ease out of his mouth.

"Hmn ... that's good. Remind you of anything, honey?" Wiping his chin off with the back of his sleeve.

Katie just looked disconcerted.

"Do you know what a BJ is? You know, a blow job?"

Katie knew, but she feigned ignorance, nodding 'no'. She thought it the safer response.

Lyle looked at her incredulous. "Just another example of our failed educational system. What are they teaching you kids these days anyway? Well, this is as good a time as any to catch up on your sex ed."

He knelt beside Katie, fingering the top of her pajama bottoms. He slowly began to pull them down around her ankles. She trembled. "Please, no, no!" she exclaimed squirming in her chair.

Katie squeezed her thighs closed but Lyle forced them apart moving his fingers slowly up the inner aspect of her thighs, higher and higher. Just before he began to touch her in that most perfect spot, *K's* admonition resurfaced – *the package must not be harmed or defiled in any way or it's your scrotum sack sewed into your mouth while you're still screaming.*

K was always over-dramatic but Lyle stopped anyway. He stood up before her. "See I can stop. I can be nice. Now it's your turn to be nice to me. I'm going to show you how to give a blowjob. So please pay attention. You just have to take a boy's, or in this case a man's penis into your mouth and suck on it as if it were a lollipop. Like this," he demonstrated by putting his index finger into his mouth and sucking on it.

"Can you do that? Lets see," he said pushing the same finger into her mouth. "Now suck on it, hard."

Katie didn't know what to do. Did she have any choice? Go along, play for time. It was the only thing to do. So she began to suck. *Playing possum!*

"Oooooh, yes! Good girl. This is going to be fun."

He unzipped his pants, reaching into his briefs to expose himself. Katie looked horrified.

Then the room exploded.

21

The crash happened so quickly that the shower of glass and splintered wood cascaded over him while his hand was still in his fly. Before he could react, he was struck powerfully in the back, stabs of pain running down his spine and back muscles. The force of the impact sent him flying past Katie, smashing his head into the corner of the cast iron stove.

He hit the floor like a dead weight. His eyes opening only momentarily. Everything fuzzy. Out of sync. Blood dripping down his face. A terrible weight pressing down on him. Slowly his consciousness ebbed into darkness.

■ ■ ■

He awoke moments later. His eyes refocusing slowly on the remains of the shattered window. Glass everywhere.

Lyle could feel his cheek resting in something wet. He touched it with his fingers. Bringing them close to his eyes, trying to focus. Blood. Slowly he began to feel the pain in his forehead. He gingerly examined the wound. Above his left eye there was a sizable welt surrounding a deep gash bleeding profusely.

He rolled over, his knees crushing glass shards beneath them. He started to push on his right hand to stand up but stopped, wincing at a sharp pain. A small sliver had stuck in the middle of his palm. He removed it, as he watched a small rivulet of blood drip from his hand.

Lyle stood up and waddled over to the sink. He took a handkerchief out of his pocket. Turning the tap, he could hear the whir of the well pump as water slowly started to gurgle, then spurt from the faucet. He wet the handkerchief in his right hand and began to dab the gash in his forehead while he held his left under the running water.

His head beginning to clear, Lyle tried to get his thoughts together. He looked around the room. She was gone.

Had someone followed him? No way or, yes, way! Must be. But how? Screw the questions, got to get her back before K arrives. If I don't, we're both fucked, but good!

Lyle began inspecting the pine floorboards. He stopped in front of one with a large knot. With his pocketknife he lifted the board up. From the opening he retrieved a metal box. He grabbed his car keys from his pants pocket. Flicking through the collection of keys he found the one to the box. He inserted it into the lock, snapping the lid open.

Inside was a Sig Sauer semi-automatic, two fully loaded clips and a box of 9 mm shells. He placed the handgun between his legs with the butt face up. He grabbed one of the clips and quickly loaded the semi-automatic. With his good right hand he shoved the handgun into the back of his waistband. He put the other clip into his pocket.

A cool breeze whipped through the partially opened front door. He felt a chill run along his neck. Lyle ran his hand on the back of his neck. There was something there, thick and gooey. He examined his hand. The mucilage like goo spread out between his fingertips. "What the fuck!"

Wiping his hand on his pant leg he started to get up when he eyed something on the floorboard he had removed. He picked up the board, closely scrutinizing it. It was blood. But the blood was almost a perfect print of a dog's paw, a very large dog. *Naw, couldn't be. How could a dog have done this?*

Was it the dogs that were trailing him? As crazy as that sounded it was the only explanation. Didn't matter though because whoever has the kid is as good as dead, reassuringly fingering the butt of his Sig Sauer.

He walked out onto the deck. Now, which way did she go?

22

Since the service station, Shelly had caught the scent and had not let go. They were moving fast now darting in and out of the scrub brush and trees that lined the roadway that closely paralleled Route 2 heading west. They had been following the scent for well over an hour when it drifted from the road they had been following and tacked off to another small one-lane road heading north. They followed this for another few miles, when suddenly, it stopped and so did they.

The two dogs began sniffing furiously along the side of the road, slowly backing up and retracing their steps. Then Shelly looked up, her right paw arched in the air, tail straight as an arrow and her nose pointing into the woods on the right hand side of the road.

Bosco quickly walked over, recognizing the smell immediately. They both headed off into the woods following the infrequently used dirt road. About a half-mile up the road they came to a clearing. A cabin loomed at them on the left just beyond the tree line. They stopped, peering about.

Darting into the woods to the left of the cabin, they made their way along the tree line until they were opposite the parked SUV. The dogs exited the woods prowling about and sniffing the vehicle. This was the one. As they came around to the rear of the vehicle they could smell her. Their den mate was here.

Both dogs then circled back around the vehicle following the tree line until they came abreast of the side of the house. Bosco rose on his hind legs and leaned against the house. He peered through the dirt-encrusted window pane. Through the open door of the room he could see the creature. While he sensed Katie he could not see her.

Bosco dropped back to the ground raising his head toward the front of the cabin. The dogs inched their way around the corner of the cabin. Shelly quietly crept on to the deck to the right of the door. Bosco stayed 10 feet off the deck. He lowered his hind legs until his butt was nearly touching the ground; his short, powerful front legs locked tightly, his head up.

With one single bound the 130-pound bullmastiff launched himself onto the deck. Bosco's front legs pounded against the dried pine surface as his hindquarters exerted incredible force propelling him into the air.

In mid leap, Bosco extended his paws bringing them down against the crossbar of the double hung window. Wood and glass shattered as he landed with a heavy thud on the cabin floor before he sprang again ramming his thick, heavily padded front paws into the creature's back.

The bullmastiff's weight and momentum sent the creature hurtling into the stove. Bosco went at him, barking with gelatinous drool flying out of his mouth. The dog appeared demonic, set to kill. He stood with his weight on his front paws resting on the creature's back. But the creature wasn't moving.

Its eyes were closed, blood flowing generously from a cut on its head.

23

Bing glanced at the van in the road. "Hey, Fitz, have two of your troopers move down toward the van on the left, along the woods. Best keep the dogs back for now," he said pointing across the road. "Ola, Leo, do the same on the other side of the road. Officer D'Amadeo, keep behind me about 10 feet and have your weapon drawn."

"OK, lets do it," Bing commanded as he moved up the road toward the van.

About 20 feet from the van, Bing with his right hand on his Glock and waving his badge and identification with the other, yelled, "FBI. Do not move. Please place both your hands outside of the driver's window. Do it now!"

The driver appeared slow to react, so Bing was about to repeat his command when the driver's hands appeared.

"Good. Thank you. Now keep them there and don't move until I tell you to do so. Is that understood?"

"Understood!" yelled the driver.

Bing kept his hand on his Glock as he approached the vehicle. "Could you please exit the vehicle," he said watching him carefully. "Now place your hands against the vehicle and spread your legs."

In a quick and practiced manner, Bing pulled the driver's legs further apart and away from the van. He expertly searched him up and down. The driver was a bit shy of six feet tall and about 160 lbs. with thinning, light graying sandy hair. He had rather delicate facial features, with a rather small nose for a man and small gray eyes, adding to his rather pasty complexion.

"You can relax now. Please turn around. What's your name?"

"Dan...Dan Clemmons. Ah ... could you tell me what this is all about?" he said with some irritation in his tone.

"Sorry about the theatrics Mr. Clemmons, but can't be too careful," he responded apologetically. "I'm SSA Ingram. We're here on a tip about a drug deal going down. We had to check you out. Just routine."

"So," Bing said gesturing to the sign on the side of the van's side panel, "you work for this Gorham Plumbing and Septic?"

"Yah," he answered trying to keep the annoyance out his voice.

"You like that work, do you?" Bing asked.

"It's a job. Do you like working for the FBI?" Clemmons said evenly.

"Not much different than cleaning out a septic tank. Get to dispose of a lot of human shit. Who wouldn't like that kind of job?"

"I guess the kind of people who you put away," he deadpanned.

"True enough, Mr. Clemmons, true enough," he chuckled. "Would you mind if I take a peek in the back?"

"Do I have a choice?" he questioned with only a hint of annoyance while Bing was already moving to the back of the van.

The rear doors were unlocked. Bing began searching inside. The usual plumber paraphernalia, including an acetylene torch, gas tank, PVC and copper piping along with a wide assortment of pipe couplings and tools. To the right of the bay was a large well-worn leather plumber's bag. Bing bent over the bag and examined it carefully. With his right hand, he removed his cell phone from his pocket, turned it on and surreptitiously dropped it into the bag.

Closing the doors, Bing thanked Clemmons for his patience and assistance. "Sorry about the hold up. Just doing our job. You can leave now and have a good day."

"Thanks," he said curtly. "…and good luck with the drug bust."

Bing stood in the middle of the road with Ola, Leo, Trish, Fitzi and the two state troopers.

"What are you thinking, Bing?" an annoyed Fitz asked.

"About this guy?"

"No, about the weather. Yah, *this guy*. Smells rotten to me. No way he's on a septic call. You think?'

"Of course, no way."

Trish looked at him quizzically. "So why'd you let him go?"

"Why indeed," Ola added.

"Because he dumped his cell," Leo interjected.

A "What?" came from both Ola and Trish.

"You didn't notice, Ola," an incredulous Leo said. "I thought you saw the boss drop his cell into the guy's plumber's bag. Right, boss?"

"Once again my very observant Dr. Watson is correct," Bing admitted with a grin.

Ola looked at Bing. "You're going to track him with your GPS?"

"No, not me," Bing said glancing at Ola and Leo. "You two are. Get back to the SUV. Follow him but not too close. Stay at least a mile off. We don't want to spook him. I want to know where he goes and whom he meets, if anyone. Wherever he lands sit on him and don't lose him. Stay with him until we find Katie, then we'll arrest this asshole."

Ola and Leo began walking down to the FBI SUV while Bing gestured to the K-9 unit to join them. He gathered together Trish, Fitzi, the Chief, the two troopers and the K-9 officers.

"We don't have the time to involve the locals. We need to act quickly so here's what we're going to do. Tom and Giselle will lead the way. I wouldn't be surprised if Katie isn't too far from here, so let's be quiet. Don't want to spook the perp. Let's go."

Bing was right. Not more than a half-mile up the overgrown road they spotted a cabin off in a clearing to the left. The K-9 officers held up Tom and Giselle who both had their hackles up. Bing huddled up the group behind the trees that lined the road.

Bing gestured toward the cabin. "Did you see the black SUV? This has to be the place. From their behavior, Tom and Giselle think so too. Here's what we're going to do."

Pointing to Fitzi and the troopers, Bing directed them to circle behind the house from the left to cover the rear and right side of the cabin. He would take Trish and the chief and come up from behind the SUV around to the front of the house.

Fitzi and his two troopers departed, entering the woods on the left and working their way along the tree line to the back of the house. Two minutes later Bing, Trish and the Chief followed their route stopping in the woods parallel to the SUV. Using the vehicle as cover they left the woods, dodged behind the SUV then slipped against the side of the house.

Bing raised his head to peer through the window. He dropped back down nodding his head to indicate that he had seen no one. The trio slipped around the corner of the house, slowly crawling on the deck, keeping below the smashed-in window. He signaled to the Chief to cover him on his left while he'd clear the right side of the cabin. Trish would provide back-up for the two. They would enter on the hand count of three.

When his third finger went up Bing burst through the opened door quickly moving his Glock from side to side as he cleared the room. The Chief did the same to his left. Trish was right behind. "Clear here," Bing yelled.

"Same here," said the Chief.

Bing gestured toward the two rooms. He took the one on the right and the Chief the left with Trish behind him. Both rooms were clear.

Moving carefully around the glass shards, Bing slowly inspected the floor. "Look over here," he said pointing to the area just to the right of the cast iron stove. He knelt down poking his index finger into the crimson stain.

Rubbing the blood between his thumb and index finger, he carefully examined the stove. "Here you can see where some-one struck the stove," gesturing to a small spot of blood on the stove's edge.

The Chief and Trish carefully backed away from the stove trying to avoid the glass on the floor and any other possible blood trace. Trish stopped suddenly, pointing with her foot at a slightly ajar floorboard.

The Chief bent down and taking a pen from his breast pocket gently lifted the board up. He looked up at Bing. "You got gloves?"

Bing took a pair from his back pocket and put them on. He removed the small metal box from beneath the floor, snapping the lid open.

"Looks like our UNSUB is now armed with a Sig Sauer P320."

"How do you know it's a Sig Sauer?" Trish asked.

"Would you believe I'm psychic? If not, how about this," he said holding up an instruction manual for a Sig Sauer P320. "There's also a box of 9 mm cartridges with most missing and no mags. Well, we best be very careful from here on."

As he was about to get up, Bing saw the bullmastiff's bloody paw print. "Looks like our canine was the one who did all this damage, probably injured the UNSUB too."

As Trish tried to carefully exit the house she called their attention to another bloody print. "This must be Katie's. Look here," as she pointed to the thinly outlined footprint.

"She must have cut her foot on a piece of glass. There's an-other one here on the deck pointing away from the road. Looks like she headed off into the woods," she said, pointing toward the tree line that marked the end of a large field of overgrown switch grass. Bing and the Chief maneuvered around the debris-strewn floor, careful not to disturb any trace evidence.

As the three stepped off the deck, Fitzi and his two troopers joined them.

"Anything?" Fitzi asked.

Bing quickly brought the troopers current on what they had found. Turning to Trish, he asked her to call Larry and request an Evidence Response Team to the cabin. "When he's done, tell him to join us. We might need him."

"Fitz, could you leave a trooper here to guard the scene and wait for our Evidence Response Team to show. Also, get a hold of your guy at the roadblock and have him ask the two local cops if either of them is familiar with these woods. If so, send him up here, pronto. Meanwhile, we best get moving with the canines," he said pointing to the woods beyond the grassy field. "Tom and Giselle should have little trouble picking up the trail."

Bing turned away for a moment staring toward the tree line. "Fitz, while you're on your cell, best call for a paramedics," he said with an anxious expression. "They can follow along as soon as they get here. We might need them."

Bing waved to the K-9 unit to join them. Trish was right. When the dogs arrived in front of the cabin, they immediately set off toward the tree line, following a path through the grass that appeared to have been recently trampled.

Just before they headed off, one of the local cops came running up the road toward them. "Hi, I'm officer Abbott," he choked out panting for breath. "They said that you could use a local who knows these woods. I do. Spent quite a bit of time as a kid running around here."

"Good," Bing said. "We can use your help."

With Bing's earlier warning still ringing in her ears, Trish withdrew her Glock, unlocked the safety and returned it to its holster.

The sun-mottled woods loomed ahead.

24

K couldn't believe his luck, or was it? Either that Feeb… what the fuck was his name, oh yah, My-Head-Up-My-Ass Ingram … was the biggest pant load since Barney Fife or he was playing him. Must be it. That Feeb was playing him. Probably has a tail on him, figuring on seeing where he goes. Well, Mr. Special Agent Fife, I'm not an asshole and I'm not fucking dumb!

"Follow this!" he yelled, giving the finger to his rear view mirror.

Convinced that the Feebs were following him, K began to use every trick in the book to evade a tail. He constantly checked his rearview mirror to see if anyone else had left the dirt road when he had. No one. He continued checking behind him to catch any vehicle trailing. None.

Using his GPS, he spotted a road on the right that ran perpendicular to the state road he was driving. Just as he approached it he sped up and made a sharp turn onto it. About 50 yards down the road he pulled over to wait. No one followed.

He continued driving the side roads, arbitrarily turning either left or right. He did this for some 20 minutes. No sign of anyone even coming close to approximating a tail. *Can't do this for much longer or I'll miss the transfer.*

K couldn't believe it. Could anyone be this lucky? He doubted it. Need to use extreme caution from here on out. Of course, he ruminated, there could be one other possibility. Maybe they snuck a tracking device into his van. That Ingram could have done it while he was searching the back of his vehicle.

With his mind racing, *K* began questioning his own theory. Sure, they could have placed some kind of tracking device in his van, if they had one. Logic would suggest that the Feebs don't carry tracking devices in their pockets on the off chance that they might run into someone who they'd like to track. Not practical.

After this heavy round of cogitation, *K* assigned his last theory to the cognitive trash bin, heavily weighted now with an enormous amount of nonsensical thoughts. Yes, indeed, rational thought led him to the obvious conclusion – the man was incompetent.

This all led him to the conclusion that he was free and clear. They had screwed up and *K* was free. Free to head back to his place outside Concord, load up the packages and head north.

Of course, the payday wouldn't be as big. But blame the bozo Lyle. Doing the math quickly in his head, he figured that instead of collecting a cool \$115,00, he'd have to settle for 40 grand. Not bad, but not the payday that he had expected. Blame Lyle.

The more he thought about Lyle, the more he was pissed off. This whole operation had been one big cluster-fuck. Who to blame: Lyle. He'd have it out with him once this was over. Yes, it was true, Lyle took all the chances and what he did required humongous gonads, a real sack load. But, still, at times, the guy was a whack job.

And now, his failed operation may cost K a big payday and almost his freedom. He decided: this would be his last joint operation with Lyle. Just too risky, he thought, as he turned onto Interstate 95, finally, heading north, to home and to complete this transaction.

As he headed north on 95, K began to think about his life and how he had come to this point. Mind you, he had no regrets. He never wanted nor asked that it be different. He knew that he had been fucked by life – by the luck of the draw. It was all about the birth lottery. Be born to the right parents, you grow up a young, outstanding man. Born to a pair of assholes, you become an asshole. Simple as that.

K was an asshole. He excelled at self-loathing. For many reasons, not all his parents doing. He also admitted that he was a pedophile and maybe that was his parents doing. He just knew one truth – he liked very young girls. They gave him the only pleasure that he could find in his rather prosaic life.

■ ■ ■

For him, it began when he was turning 14. A year of continuous nocturnal emissions. Everything, it seemed, sexual, exciting and, bewildering. So bewildering – especially Deidre.

She was just 6 when he first met her. She was a cousin on his mother's side. Mom would visit her sister, Margaret, every month back then and began taking *K* along with her just to keep an eye on him.

Deidre was adorable. Slender, with beautiful facial features that were a portent of the beautiful young woman that she would become. Her lips especially, even at such a young age appeared to be those of a mature woman, plump and ripe. Blue eyes and a small straight nose all framed in a luscious cascade of liquid gold curls. He remembered all of her and the thought still excited him.

Deidre liked to play house. Initially, *K* would have no part of it but mom insisted.

"Come on dear, amuse the child while mommy and auntie talk. Be a good boy and we'll stop for ice cream on our way home."

So he did as he was bid. But not for the ice cream, certainly a nice benefit, he did it to keep his mother off his back. She could bitch and bitch, and just make your life a misery if you didn't do what she wanted you to do. And, as the only child, he was the sole target of her ire since dad was smart; he hid out at the local bar.

Deidre took *K* by the hand and led him up stairs to her bedroom. It was a very feminine, frilly affair. She spent the next 10 minutes setting up her tea set on a small table with two small chairs. When she had finished, she sat down and asked *K* to join her. "Please sit," she said with a great degree of maturity. "Now, you are the daddy and I'm the mommy. And we'll have some tea before you go off to work to make money. OK?"

With a frown K sat down and picked his cup from the saucer and drank his imaginary tea. All the while, he stared at her. For reasons, even today, he could not understand why, she captivated his attention. She was so pretty and beguiling for someone so young.

After five minutes of drinking the imaginary brew, Deidre put her cup down and announced, "Well, the tea is all gone and it is time for you to go to work, dear." She then stood up, bent over the table and kissed K on the mouth, a brief, wet kiss. A young innocent girl's kiss, but one that he received far differently. It had excited him.

Deidre asked him to go out into the hall, close the door and wait for her. "OK," she said through the door. "Please knock on the door now." K did as he was told.

She opened the door and threw her arms around him rubbing her body against him and kissing him first on the cheek and then the mouth. "Welcome home," she giggled. She seemed to hold firmly to him forever, while he grew more and more excited, until like a giant ocean wave, it cascaded over him, through him, around him, swirling into a whirlpool of such extraordinary pleasure that his whole being seemed to be focused on that one point below his belt.

K pushed her aside and turned toward the door. "I have to go to the bathroom!" He rushed out of the room to the bathroom at the far end of the corridor. He was a mess. His ejaculate had leaked through his briefs and stained his pants. He spent the next 15 minutes cleaning himself while Deidre waited patiently outside the bathroom door.

"When are you coming out," she pleaded. "You've been in there a long time. We aren't finished playing house yet."

When *K* came out he lied to Deidre claiming that he had accidentally spilled some water on his pants when he was washing his hands. Grateful that he was finally out of the bathroom, Deidre dismissed his explanation out of hand. "Come on, we should have another cup of tea and then do some housework."

His relationship with this precocious 6-year-old would last for nearly two years. Then she and her family moved. He had searched to ride that wave for all his life, but he had yet to find it.

That one and first sexual experience had imprinted itself on his subconscious and would forever inform his sexual proclivities. He could change nothing. No talk therapy, drug or punishment, however grievous, would change what he had become. It was what it was.

These thoughts raced through his mind, draining away into his subconscious as he turned on to Interstate 89.

25

Katie's feet were killing her. Her left especially painful. The glass cut in the sole continued to bleed and sting, more so every time it hit the ground. To limit the pain, she began favoring the foot, putting more pressure on her right, causing that foot to begin to ache.

With bound wrists and sore feet, running was torturous. The path through the hardwood forest was overgrown with a lush carpet of ferns. They disguised a forest floor crisscrossed with decaying tree limbs, stumps and protruding roots. More than once she yelped in pain as her toes banged into a hidden obstruction.

In the lead, carefully threading her way along the path, Shelly could sense Katie's difficulty and began to shorten her stride. While the lab kept her nose at shoulder height, she continued to sample the air moist with dew and the sweet smell of woodland decay. Odorous traces of white tail deer, coyotes, raccoon, rabbit and opossum flit across her path. All were ignored. Only one was sought – the one that would alert her to the creature.

Bosco followed. He kept about 10 feet behind Katie, his head on a constant swivel to the left, right, and behind. Continuously on guard should the creature appear. His ponderous gait interrupted by an occasional limp caused by his injured right paw. An inner toe pad had been badly cut when he had landed on the glass-covered cabin floor.

Katie glanced ahead as she watched Shelly nimbly pick her way along the path. They began to slowly climb a ridge densely covered with oak, maple, an occasional black cherry and stands of birch. The path now becoming even more obstructed from fallen forest debris.

As Katie began watching the path immediately to her front, to avoid stumbling, she suddenly bumped into a silent, stilled Shelly.

"What's the matter, girl, see something?" she asked with her mouth close to the Lab's ear. Looking up, she saw what Shelly saw, a deep ravine with a stream running through it. Further to the right, at the bottom of the ravine, some enterprising hiker had placed a tree trunk across the stream to serve as a rather crude bridge.

Since the stream looked rather shallow, maybe a foot or two, she decided to wade across, hoping the cold water would soothe her painful feet. She urged Shelly to descend the ravine that dropped 30 feet to the stream. Shelly easily made her way down as Bosco waited for Katie to descend.

Without the use of her arms, Katie was finding it difficult to descend the treacherously slippery, steep embankment. A third of the way down she lost her footing, falling on her butt and sliding feet first down the slope. Sensing her danger, Bosco charged to her side barking wildly while trying to stop her fall by grabbing her pajama top with his mouth. The force of his tugging pulled Katie onto her side, her feet swinging almost parallel to her body. As the torque pulled her pajamas free of Bosco's teeth, she began to roll uncontrollably down the embankment with the bullmastiff running beside her.

Suddenly, Bosco jumped in front of Katie in an attempt to stop her rolling when he lost purchase on the dew-wet slope. He rolled back on his hindquarters as the girl banged into him. In a jumble, the two went rolling down the last 10 feet of slope into the streambed.

Katie landed head first into the icy, cold water. She quickly rolled on her side to lift her head out of the water choking and gasping for air. Once she had her breath back, she sat for a moment in the cool refreshing water. She looked to her left to see Bosco emerge from the stream, soaked and a bit disgruntled. He stood looking at her then began to violently shake his thick, waterlogged, tawny coat. The water flew off him in a series of ever diminishing spirals, thoroughly wetting Shelly who wandered too close to the drenched bullmastiff.

Katie couldn't help but laugh at the bedraggled condition of the three. She gathered herself up on her knees, pausing momentarily to enjoy, if only for a few moments more, the palliative effect of the water on her body. Every part of her ached. Her feet, legs and arms were a mass of bruises, small scrapes and cuts, and her wrists, now deeply lacerated by the plastic thongs that held them secure.

She stood up and made her way across the stream. The slope on the other side was just as steep as the one she and Bosco had tumbled down. Intuitively, Shelly began leading the group along the stream bank until they came to a fallen oak. The stream had undermined the tree's root ball causing it to collapse. The thick exposed roots provided ample foot holds for Katie to climb to the top of the root ball. From there she managed to gingerly step down onto the embankment. The dogs quickly followed.

Shelly resumed her lead position, moving in a northwesterly direction to interdict the path they had been following. She began to bob her head from ground to air, air to ground, searching for the smell of deer, a particular group of white tail. It had been easy for Shelly to follow the overgrown trail once they left the cabin because the deer made use of it as they traversed the heavily wooded forest. Once the lab recognized their strong smell she knew she was back on course. In less than five minutes, she had identified the trail.

They had traveled perhaps another mile when the path divided. Shelly began to take the path on the right when Katie told her to stop. She stood for a moment trying to decide which way to go. The right hand path continued on a gentle ascent while the left began a descent. Logic told her that a road or a residence would more likely be found going down rather than up. She gestured to Shelly with a nod to take the left path. So they did. And that, it turned out, made all the difference.

The path descended sharply into a bowl that formed the saddle between two heavily wooded hills. The trail continued across the bowl into the woods at the base of the opposite hill.

Katie began to question both her logic and decision. But we're here, she thought, and nothing to do but push on.

As she descended the hill, Katie's thoughts of doubt brought to mind another of her father's favorite adages, "It doesn't matter what decision you make but that you *do* make a decision. Indecision kills faster than no decision at all." She had made her decision and they would live with it.

A half-hour later, Shelly stopped, peering into the light ahead of her. Up until now the path had been heavily shaded by the thick canopy of leaves spreading out toward the sky from the numerous trees populating the wood. Katie looked past Shelly to see an open patch of cloudless cerulean blue. The path ahead now appeared like a tunnel leading to an open space.

They moved hurriedly, the three of them exiting the thick wood to a suddenly barren cliff scape. To her left and right, large slabs of granite stood testimony to the bygone labor of hundreds of stoneworkers. She peered across the abyss that stood in front of them. It was a large pit, perhaps 150 yards in diameter. Its bottom a large pool of water the color of verdigris rimmed with granite debris.

The path ended here. There was no way out but the way they came. Katie stood for a moment, catching her breath. Turning toward the two dogs, she nodded toward the woods. "Come, we need to go back."

Shelly looked at her, cocking her head to the side, as if to say "What?"

"Sorry girl," Katie said apologetically. "I was wrong. We should have gone your way so we have to backtrack. Come, let's go!"

Reluctantly, the band set off into the tunnel of trees, dappled with sunlight filtering through the towering canopy of leaves. Shelly took her usual position about 20 feet in front of Katie. They had only gone 50 yards or so when Shelly stopped. The lab stood rigid, her front left leg curled toward her chest, her hackles up and her tail straight in the air. Katie could hear a low growl boiling up from deep inside her.

"What's the matter, girl? See something?"

Kneeling beside Shelly she peered down the path. Bosco trotted up beside her, his heavy breathing clearly audible, drool spilling from his jowls. He began to growl, a growl that soon erupted into a full-blown bark.

The creature had come into view.

26

Lyle had been making good time, nimbly making his way along the deer track. From the time he entered the woods, he had decided that his only option was to follow the clearly visible trace, something he assumed the girl would do. She had no other options.

He had followed the track for nearly an hour when he came to a gulley formed by a stream running at its bottom. A few feet to his left, he noticed that the slope leading down to the stream had been recently disturbed. On closer inspection he could see two foot prints clearly visible near the top of the slope. It had to have been the girl. Then farther down the slope he saw another print, nearly the size of his fist. It belonged to a dog, a very large dog.

Lyle edged his way carefully down the gully's slippery slope. At the bottom he knelt by the stream, putting his cupped hand into the cold water, splashing it on his face. He was sweating and the water felt good. He was getting closer. He could feel it.

He made his way up the steep embankment. At the top he scanned the underbrush for the deer track. It was just a few feet to his right. As he entered the track he picked up his pace. If he could close in on them soon, he might still be able to make his meet with K. If he couldn't, he'd make the delivery himself but he'd have to call K first. Only K knew where the drop-off was.

The people who ran the network were very careful. Just like a terrorist organization, they organized the network into cells each operating independently. Moreover, the operatives in each cell only knew the contact in the next link in the network's chain. So Lyle knew K and K knew, well K knew whomever K delivered the packages to, and so on and so on. Very smart. In that way, the money guys at the top were insulated. So everything now depended on him getting a hold of K once he bagged the girl and killed those friggin' dogs. Because without K, there was no payday.

■ ■ ■

This was the seventh job for the network. It had been a very lucrative relationship. From his cut of the contracts, Lyle had been able to squirrel away nearly $1 million. When he got paid for delivering the girl, he'd go well over that. He had decided sometime ago that once he topped a mil, he'd call it quits. Figured he'd retire to Thailand.

When he mentioned retirement to Thailand, K had looked at him quizzically. "Why Thailand?" he had asked rather incredulously. Lyle told him about a vacation he had taken there about five years ago. He had gone to Thailand not for its culture, but for its sexual openness.

As part of a sex tour, 80 guys paid four grand apiece to experience all the perversions Bangkok had to offer and there were many. It was where Lyle could indulge his penchant for very young girls without fear of either being arrested or shamed as a social pariah. Sex any way you wanted it, with whomever you wanted it, whenever you wanted it – boys, girls, men, women, gay, straight, transvestites, transgender, transsexual. You choose. Yup, Thailand! There he had had his fill of very young girls, none older than 14. It was nirvana. That was the place, a place where with one mil in the kitty you could live like a sheikh.

■ ■ ■

Lyle could feel the early morning spring chill slowly dissipate as the sun grew higher in the sky. It would have been a pleasant early morning hike if not for the business at hand.

Up ahead he could see the track split with the one on the right heading higher and the other lower. Which did she take? He stopped for a moment to consider his decision. What would she have done? Logic, he mused, would argue for her heading to the left in anticipation of finding a road or people. But since when were young girls logical. Though this young thing seemed more together than most. Had the guts and good sense to break for it when she had the chance. Whoever bought her was going to have his hands full.

Lyle made his decision. He took the track to the left.

27

Ola and Leo had been sitting on *K's* house for half hour following an hour and a half on the road. *K* hadn't budged since they began observing him. Ola had contacted Bing as soon as they began the surveillance and asked him to arrange for a court order to tap his phones. They had just received the OK.

Their SUV was parked at an oblique angle to the house about fifty yards from K's driveway. They had been observing with Canon binoculars. While Ola stared through the Canon, Leo was staring at her.

"What are you looking at?" Ola said wryly.

"I'm staring at Super-Special Agent Ola Dabrowski, without a doubt the most beau…I mean the most competent agent in the Bureau."

"It's OK, Leo. You can say I'm beautiful. Gorgeous, in fact. Make that *drop dead gorgeous*. It's true. So live with it." She stared at him smirking. "It's difficult being the most gorgeous female agent in the Bureau but I bear my good looks without shame or complaint."

"I understand completely," Leo retorted obsequiously. "I have the same cross to bear."

"What?" Ola smirked. "You think you're the *most* gorgeous woman in the Bureau?"

"Hardly. I'm the most gorgeous *man* in the Bureau."

"Did you pass your last psych review?" she giggled.

"No. The shrink claimed I was just besot, bewildered and beguiled, and wanted to know who the woman was," he deadpanned.

Shaking her head, Ola returned to peering through the binoculars. "Uh, oh. The garage door is opening."

"What's he doing?" Leo asked.

"Can't tell from here."

"Should we get closer?"

"Not a good idea. Don't want to get made."

"So we follow?" Leo asked.

"Yup, we follow," she said turning to Leo. "Get on your cell and fill Bing in on what's happening. Oh, and remember, Bing's cell is in the subject's vehicle so call Fitz not Bing."

"Gotcha!"

While *K* backed out of the driveway, lowering the garage door as he exited on to the street, Ola waited as Leo put his call through to Fitz.

"Hi, Captain. Is Bing available?"

A moment later Bing was on Fitzi's cell. "Leo, what's up?"

"Bing, Elvis has left the building. We assume you want us to follow."

"Yes, keep on him. I'm expecting that he'll be heading upstate so I'll have Larry notify Boston to have more agents sent your way and the staties up there to coordinate with you. Keep me informed and be careful. We know our UNSUB is armed so yours might be too."

"Will do," Leo said shutting off his cell and turning to Ola. "Continue to follow wherever he goes. See where it takes us. Larry will request back up from the field office and coordinate with the New Hampshire staties."

Ola turned onto the road, checking the laptop that lay on the console between her and Leo. "There he is," she said pointing to the red blip on the screen. "We'll stay about a quarter mile behind until we get in the open then we'll drop back to a mile or so."

"Let's rock n' roll, partner!"

28

With the sun at its zenith, Bing's group moved hurriedly to keep pace with Tom and Giselle. The dogs were on a tear, moving quickly through the woodland's thick underbrush. Their noses attuned to the multiple scents of their prey.

The dogs only halted momentarily when they came to the gulley sheltering the stream. They stood at the edge of the gully's steep slope for just an instant before plunging head first down into and across the stream then up the other side. Their handlers worked mightily trying to restrain their enthusiasm.

Bing was behind Trish as she gingerly navigated her way down the gully's slope. At the bottom she scampered through the chilly stream as quickly as she could. On the other bank she looked for a handhold to help her climb the steep embankment. Finding an exposed tree root, she grabbed hold and pulled herself up. She planted her right foot into the soft earth then her left momentarily releasing her grip on the root. She quickly lost purchase with her right and then left foot, spilling backwards against Bing.

Bing tried to grab her as she fell against his chest, but he was off balance. He came crashing down into the stream with Trish on top of him. The weight of her had knocked the wind out of him. Gasping for air, he tried to pull himself out of the streambed's cold water that was flash freezing his manhood.

On his knees he started to get his breath as Fitzi grabbed him by the shoulders, lifting him up. Trish was still on her butt.

"Well I can see that chivalry is dead," she said acerbically.

"Not quite," Larry said offering a hand, "just among the senior officers."

Standing on the embankment wiping himself off, Bing looked around somewhat embarrassed. "Alright, enough of the lap dances, let's move."

Turning to Trish, who was peeling her wet pants away from her curvaceous butt, Bing said in a low voice, "You could kill a man with that thing."

"Then don't tailgate," she said smiling.

The sun was moving higher in the sky, shooting shafts of light into the woods. The early morning dew and chill had dissipated, the air growing warmer and more humid. When the party stopped momentarily at the fork in the deer track, Tom and Giselle took brief sniffs to the right then immediately turned dragging their handlers to the left toward the ridge.

As they descended into the saddle between the two ridges, the air grew cooler and then began to warm again as they pushed back up the other side. Nearly to the top of the ridgeline, the dogs and handlers suddenly stopped. One of the handlers turned and looked back to Bing gesturing with his hand to listen.

They all stood quiet for a moment then they heard it—the unmistakable crack of a gunshot. "Gunfire" Bing yelled, immediately shooting forward in a run, waving everybody on.

29

Lyle watched as the girl and the two dogs turned and ran back toward the break of light at the end of the forest arbor. He didn't rush. He knew that where they were going was a dead end. Their dead end. The hunt was over.

Walking at a leisurely pace, Lyle retrieved his Sig Sauer from his rear waistband, unlocking the safety and chambering a round. He would take his time. No need to rush. He would enjoy this, especially blowing the heads off those two dogs. Maybe he'd do it in front of the girl just to make a point.

As he stepped out of the woods into the sun-splashed ledge, he saw the girl huddled at the far end with the chocolate lab.

"Well, well missy, nice to see you again. Miss me?" The words spilling from his lips with obvious venom. "You caused me mucho problemas, you little bitch. Someone has got to pay for that inconvenience."

Lyle looked directly at the lab standing next to Katie. "Yup, I think the perfect penance for you would be to watch me blow that dog's head off. How 'bout that? Hey missy?"

He waved the gun at the girl. "Best move aside. Not that I'd hit you, but you don't want the dog's brains splattered all over you. Do you?"

Lyle raised the gun, taking careful aim at the lab. Shelly stood there watching him, a low growl emitting from deep inside her. About to pull the trigger, Katie stepped in front of the dog.

"Please, don't kill her," she pleaded. "I promise to be good. I won't run away again. I promise, but don't hurt her, please."

"Too late little missy," he said lowering the gun slightly.

He looked Katie in the eye while grabbing his groin. "You'll behave because if you don't you'll get this in spades. Now that I think of it, you'll get this anyway. You owe me big time. If it hadn't been for that…hey where is that…"

Lyle's unasked question was answered with a thunderous bark. He turned to look behind him but too late. The bullmastiff was on him.

In one quick leap, Bosco plowed into Lyle's chest, his paws raking downward while his enormous jaws tore into his right shoulder. Lyle screamed in pain falling to the floor of the granite ledge. He came down hard, the impact sending the Sig Sauer flying from his hand.

Lyle quickly rolled over toward his right to reach the gun lying some 10 feet away. He started scrambling along the ledge when Bosco pounced again coming down forcefully on his back, smashing Lyle's chest into the hard granite.

Lyle was fighting for breath with the bullmastiff standing over him with his right paw on the middle of his back and the other pressed against Lyle's left arm. The pain from the fractured arm was excruciating. Lyle let out a grunt. He reached down with his right hand to grab the hunting knife strapped to his ankle.

Pulling the knife free of its scabbard, Lyle swung it behind his back raking Bosco's rib cage with a deep cut. The dog yelped with pain momentarily releasing his victim.

Free of the dog, Lyle lunged for the Sig Sauer. He was about to grab it when Katie came leaping over him, attempting to kick the gun over the ledge. Lyle reached up, grabbing her left foot sending her stumbling to the ground. Her shoulder smashed into the gun sending it a few feet closer to the cliff edge.

Lyle managed to crab walk the remaining few feet to retrieve the Sig Sauer. He stood up and turned toward Bosco.

Katie yelled "No!" while whipping her leg at the back of Lyle's left knee catching it with the top of her foot.

The impact collapsed the knee and Lyle lost his balance. He whipped around with his left hand smashing into Katie's face. She screamed as Lyle, choked with pain, watched his left hand dangle from the wrist.

"Bitch," he screamed as he turned to Bosco. The dog got back on his feet. His huge, black coal eyes opened wide with saliva-covered jowl's flared, exposing enormous canines.

Lyle fired off a round a bit wide as the 9 mm tore through the tip of Bosco's right ear. The dog howled in pain. As he was about to fire another round and finish the job, he heard a shrieking bark accompanied by a searing pain that ran from just above his right ankle to his thigh. He looked down to see the lab's jaws ensnared in his pant leg. He whipped the gun around and fired wildly, the bullet piercing the top of the dog's hip and clipping the tail.

The bullet's impact sent Shelly twisting to the ground, turning her head to watch her hindquarters twitch.

With the lab down, Lyle turned back to Bosco. But in a stunning imitation of a defensive lineman's bull rush, the bull-mastiff plowed into Lyle headfirst. The blow sent him stumbling back fighting to maintain his balance. If he went down the bullmastiff would be on him and it would be game, set, and match. He began to steady himself as his left foot came down on solid footing. While the right made purchase with his toes, the heel found nothing but air. Lyle started to slip backwards. Instinctively, his useless left hand reached for something to grab but only managing to flop back and forth as if waving to a crowd, his right still holding the Sig Sauer. Then as if in slow motion he began to fall over the edge.

As Lyle fell, he spent the last two seconds of his life recalling what had brought him to this end. His one dominating thought focused on the nearly $1 million he had in the bank and that he would never have the chance to spend. That thought and the image of that manic dog were the last of his life.

When Lyle's back smashed into one of the numerous granite slabs lining the rim of the quarry pool, the impact snapped his head up, then back, fracturing his skull. The fracture began immediately oozing blood, serous fluid and brain matter on to the granite surface, like a cracked egg poured onto a griddle.

What remained of Lyle Stembeck seeped onto the warm stone forming a perfect halo around his head.

Bosco remained at the edge of the ledge, looking down. Knots of saliva, tinged pink from his and Lyle's blood, hung in thin spaghetti-like strips, slowly stretching until one by one they broke away, landing gently on the corpse below.

30

With his gun drawn, Bing broke out of the woods and onto the ledge. He began to sweep the area with his Glock as the others joined him. But no UNSUB. The group spread out across the ledge checking to ensure the UNSUB was not hiding among the granite slabs.

Bing rushed over to Katie. "Hi Katie, my name is Bing Ingram. I'm with the FBI." He kneeled down next to her, tears welling up in her eyes. "Don't be afraid. You're safe now."

"You're a very brave girl, Katie. You've had a long and frightening day. So if you want to cry go ahead and cry," he said seeing her teary eyes. "You deserve to."

Katie looked up at him, holding back the tears. "That man, he shot my dogs," she said looking toward the edge of the ledge. "He shouldn't have shot my dogs. They were only trying to protect me."

"I know, Katie. I know. They're two very brave canines. Now let's see about getting your hands free." Bing took out his pocketknife and cut the plastic restraining bands off her wrists. They must have hurt. The wrists were raw and bloody.

"Hey, Fitzi, how far away are the medics?"

"About 10 minutes or so."

Bing turned back to the girl. "We'll have someone here to help you in a few minutes."

The two dog handlers commanded Tom and Giselle to sit. Grateful for the break, both sat and nuzzled each other as the handlers walked over to Bing.

"We've both got first aid kits," offered one of the handlers as he walked toward Bing. "We can bandage her up and also take a look at the dogs."

"Thanks," Bing said. "Her wrists do look pretty raw."

While one handler attended to Katie's wrists the other tended to Shelly.

Trish walked over and sat next to the girl. She gently turned Katie's face toward hers.

"Hmm, you have a bad bruise on your face. Did the man who abducted you do that?"

"Yah, when I tried to kick the gun away. He punched me in the face."

"Well he won't be doing that to anyone anymore." Trish looked at Bing and gestured to the cliff edge. "He's over there."

Bing got up and walked over to where Fitzi and the Chief were standing. He peered over the edge to see Lyle Stembeck's crumpled body lying in a pool of blood. Kneeling beside the chief, he stared at the body for a moment.

"So," asked the chief, "was it that big brute of a dog that got him?"

"No," Bing mused looking back at Trish holding Katie in her arms. "It wasn't the dog…it was beauty killed the beast."

The chief looked confused. "Wha'?"

Fitzi smiled and whispered in the chief's ear. "I'll explain later."

31

Within a few minutes, the paramedics arrived with a stretcher. They immediately attended to Katie. After a brief exam, the female paramedic informed Bing that the girl seemed fine except for being dehydrated and suffering a few minor foot, face, and leg cuts and abrasions, none serious. They redressed the wounds and started an IV and began a saline solution drip to address the dehydration.

Before leaving, Bing asked Fitzi for his cell phone and to leave a trooper to guard the crime scene until the Evidence Response Team arrived. Walking over to Katie, Bing knelt beside her.

"We're going to call your parents and let them know you're alright. Would you like to talk to them?"

"Yes, please," her face brightening. "They must be very upset."

Bing waved Trish over, handing her Fitzi's cell. "As first responder, maybe you'd like the privilege of calling the parents."

Trish took the phone gingerly. "Yes, I would. I'd like that very much," smiling gratefully at him.

As the rescue party all watched, Trish dialed the Gaines home. A police officer answered. "Hi, Fric…oh, Frac," she smiled lightly. "We found Katie and she's fine. Let me talk to the parents."

Officer Fracelli turned with the phone in his hand and a big grin on his face. "Mr. and Mrs. Gaines, they found her safe and sound!"

Martin ran over and grabbed the phone. "She's OK. She's not hurt, is she?"

"No Mr. Gaines, your daughter is fine. She's a real trooper. She'd like to talk to you and Mrs. Gaines," Trish said handing the phone to a delighted Katie.

Liz Gaines moved next to her husband pressing her head against the receiver.

"Katie, Katie! Are you OK? That man didn't hurt you, did he?"

"Just a few bumps and bruises, nothing serious," she said cheerily.

"Oh, thank God you're safe. We love you so much, honey. So very much. Come home as quickly as you can. Can't wait to hug you." Liz said crying softly as she buried her head into Martin's shoulder.

Holding his wife, Martin repositioned the phone to his other ear. "I love you babe. Come home to us."

"I love you too," Katie responded pausing for a moment. "Dad, remember what you told me? If ever I was in trouble to run the first chance I had and to keep on running. Well, that's what I did dad." Tears began welling up in her eyes. "I ran and ran and ran."

"That's my little girl, my brave little girl," he said with tears rolling down his cheeks.

Teary eyed, Katie handed the cell back to Trish. "Mr. Gaines, Officer D'Amadeo, here ... Yes, sir, you're very welcome. Well it was a real group effort. Local, State and the FBI. We had a great team, some luck and four dogs who led the way. Yup, four dogs. Tom and Giselle, the search and rescue dogs, and your neighbor's dogs, Shelly and Bosco. They're the real heroes. Without them we would have never found Katie and, in the end, it was Shelly and Bosco who rescued her."

"We'll be taking Katie to a hospital for a brief checkup. We'll let you know where you can meet us once we're on the road. See you soon." Trish clicked off, raising her hand to Bing.

"Need to make one more call," she said.

Trish then dialed the Capellos.

32

They had been driving for an hour and a half heading in a northerly direction, generally following the Connecticut River that formed a natural boundary between New Hampshire and Vermont. Leo glanced over to Ola. "So, whadya think? Where's this guy headed?"

"Beats me." Ola shook her head. "Only thing I can think of is that he's doing what Bingo said he'd probably do, rendezvous with someone at a small private airport. Fly the goods out."

"Yah, I was thinking that even though he missed the connection with the UNSUB, he probably already had a kid or two stashed at his place ready for delivery." Leo opened his smartphone and went online.

"What are you doing? Checking out porno sites!"

"Now why would I do that when I have you sitting next to me?"

"Don't be fresh. What are you looking for?"

'Well," Leo explained, "I thought I'd check out small civilian airports in New Hampshire to see if there are any in the general direction we're headed."

"You know, Leo, that's such a good idea you must have stole it from me." She broke a soft grin eyeing him.

Leo held his smartphone in his left hand, while his right flipped through an Atlas of New England. He turned to a page with a blowup of northern New Hampshire. "There are two in this direction," he said turning from his cell to the map. "Both small, private airports with relatively light traffic, probably mostly summer residents and hunters."

Within a few miles, they had passed one and the other was not too far ahead and to the east, Mt. Washington airport. "I'm getting the feeling that he's not headed toward an airfield." She shook her head looking over at Leo.

"Think you're right." Leo scratched his head and began examining the map again in earnest. "You know, maybe its not an airfield we should be looking for. Maybe it's a lake."

"What?' Ola said, squinting her eyes.

"How do hunters and residents this far north get here?"

"Seaplanes!"

"Yes, my Illuminata! Seaplanes!"

Leo increased his perusal of the map while Ola began focusing on the terrain. They were now traveling along Route 3 roughly continuing to parallel the Connecticut River. To the left she could see the verdant Green Mountains of Vermont and on her right the White Mountains of New Hampshire, both part of the huge Appalachian chain that ran along the east coast. Carved by retreating glaciers eons ago, they formed solid walls of rolling hills and mountains that framed both sides of Route 3.

Up ahead, slightly to the north and on her left, Ola could see the bulging presence of the 2800-foot, Monadnock Mountain. It stood majestically just over the border in Vermont. The mountain also stood at the apex of a long, verdant corridor of lush woodland and gently rolling hills – a natural habit for abundant wildlife – that stretched down to northern Connecticut.

Ola recalled seeing a satellite nighttime image of what geologists called the eastern uplands. It appeared as a large, dark finger seemingly untouched by human habitation. The uplands were framed to the east by the faint light of the Boston-Providence megalopolis and to the west by the glittering necklace of light from cities along the Connecticut.

Her enjoyment of the magnificent scenery was jostled by Leo's voice, "He's turning!"

"Where's he heading," Ola asked.

"Nor by nor' east."

"OK, Captain Ahab, what road?"

"He's taking a left on to Route 145 in Colebrook a few miles ahead. It's a small one-laner. Takes you to Pittsburg ... New Hampshire, not PA."

"What the hell is up there?"

"Lakes, that's what. Lakes!"

They made their way through Colebrook, a quaint, neat little New England village with its brightly colored storefronts lining the main street. The road out of Colebrook was narrow, winding its way through thinly cut valleys that bordered an escarpment of the White Mountains. While the scenery was beautiful, there was little evidence of civilization until you reached Pittsburg.

Outside Pittsburg, the red dot that marked Clemmons' van veered off of 145 on to Cedar Stream Road. "What's he doing now?"

"I think this is the place. The road parallels Lake Francis. It's big."

"But where would a seaplane land and dock?"

Leo held up a hand to Ola, gesturing for her to wait a moment. He began fiddling with his smartphone. "I think he's headed right there." Leo pointed to a satellite close up of the south shore of Lake Francis showing a large jetty jutting out into the lake. "Lets follow the bouncing dot and see if that's where he's headed."

Cedar Stream followed the south shore of Lake Francis with large, towering 1600-to-2000-foot hills bordering it on the right. Two miles down the road the red dot turned on to an access road headed toward the shore. The road terminated at the jetty. "Gotcha!" Leo exclaimed.

"Sometimes, you amaze me," Ola admitted, amusingly.

■ ■ ■

Ola pulled the SUV up to the side of the road at the entrance to the access road. "How far behind us are the others?"

Leo got on the cell with both the staties and the two agents from the Boston field office. "They're both about 10 minutes out."

"We probably should wait for backup, but if that plane has already landed then these kids could be gone before we get to them." She looked pensive for a moment. Turning to Leo, she said, "Leo, we better…."

Leo interrupted her. "I know, let's do it. Fuck'em!"

"You're my kind of guy, Leo."

Ola had Leo called both the staties and the agents to let them know that they should join them as soon as possible and that because of exigent circumstances, they were proceeding to apprehend the perps. They got out of the SUV and walked to the rear of the vehicle. They discarded their FBI jackets and donned their bulletproof vests, checked their weapons, and proceeded down the access road.

The dirt access road was well compacted, no ruts and evidently well used. At the end of the road was a clearing that opened to the lake. To the right was an old, weathered cabin painted a faded red. The slightly ajar front door was blue, the peeling paint nearly extinct. The side of the building facing the road had a window with one pane missing, covered with a piece of rotting cardboard. Next to the window was a tall pole supporting electrical and telephone lines strung to another pole half way down the access road. Clemmons' van was parked on the left near the woods, directly across from the cabin's front entrance.

Beyond the cabin the clearing opened to lake frontage. A low stonewall ran along the shorefront as erosion protection. Jutting out from the wall was a 60-foot-long aluminum dock shaped like a T.

Ola looked back at Leo gesturing him to follow her into the woods. They eased forward to the edge of the clearing facing the side of the cabin with the window. A low hum began to spread across the lake as Clemmons emerged from the cabin.

Ola nudged Leo, pointing in the air to a small dark speck in the brilliant blue sky. "There, can you see it?"

As the speck grew closer its details became more discernable. It was a white, red-striped Cessna Caravan Amphibian. "Hell, that's at least a 10-seater. What are they expecting to airlift out of here," Leo whispered. They watched as Clemmons walked toward the dock, his right hand above his eyes blocking the glare of the sun.

The Cessna came in low passing a mere 50 feet above the dock then turning left in a long swooping curve. The plane now grew smaller as it approached the dam at the west end of the lake. The pilot descended slowly. About a quarter mile from the dock he began his landing approach, the pontoons striking the glassy surface of the lake, bouncing only briefly then settling gently down onto the water. The seaplane set down about a quarter of a mile beyond the dock quickly turning toward the far shore where Clemmons stood.

With its propeller still turning, the seaplane nimbly approached the dock, the right pontoon gently nudging the top of the T. Clemmons walked to the end of the dock waving at the occupants. A man exited the passenger side. Dressed in khakis, a black tee and a black leather jacket, he gestured to Clemmons to throw him the rope curled up on the dock. He grabbed the rope, securing it to a ring on top of the pontoon, while Clemmons fastened it to the dock cleats.

The man jumped on to the dock and joined Clemmons, chatting while they walked to the van.

Ola and Leo watched them intently.

33

K stood on the dock watching the Cessna make its wide arc in preparation for landing. Good, he thought, be out of here in 15 minutes. He was anxious. This contract had been a fiasco from the git-go. Lyle had really screwed up. He might have to seriously reconsider his arrangement with that imbecile. Didn't like him anyway. He knew Lyle didn't much care for him either. Good riddance. He wasn't worth the time or aggravation.

A big problem though – dumping him. Finding some one to replace Lyle would be difficult. The kid had cojones. No doubt about it.

Thinking of Lyle brought *K* to thinking about Syl. Funny how the brain works. One thought leads to another then another. All related in some perverse, neurological way.

It was Syl who was responsible for bringing him here. To this time. To this place.

■ ■ ■

K and Syl, had been close, if for no other reason than their common love of pre-pubescent girls. They had met at Goudlet's Video, which everyone pronounced "Good Lays". Buddy Goudlet held a swap meet every other Wednesday night in the basement of his business. It was for special clients – those who enjoyed hard-core porn, especially child porn.

K had an extensive collection of child porn, none more interesting than those he had filmed himself. He had a nine-year-old sequestered in a hidden room in his basement. There she performed for him. He filmed every moment they spent together. Everything that they did. Every sexual, erotic act.

When Syl saw the videos, he went bonkers. He couldn't get enough. He tried to trade three for one but *K* held out. Got six for one. Syl still thought he got the better of the deal.

That had been the beginning. Soon, Syl's appetite had been whetted. So they had begun trading sex partners, girls they had abducted or bought. It proved a profitable arrangement for both. Dramatically cut down their procurement costs. It was also safer. There was less need for abducting a girl off the streets. Always dicey and dangerous.

One day, about 10 years ago, *K* got a call from Syl.

"Hi, there. Whadsup?"

"I've been sick, *K*. Don't know what the fuck is going on with me. Feel real crappy. Seeing my doc tomorrow."

"Sorry to hear. Anything I can do?" Truth be told, *K* didn't give a damn.

"Actually, that's why I'm calling. I have this little side thing going. A nice piece of business that pays well. But I'm not up to it. Not the way I feel."

"So what can I do?"

"I've got a proposition for you K. I deliver packages for some people. Very important packages and they pay real well. I need to deliver this package up to northern New Hampshire. You'll get twenty grand for your trouble. Be about a two and half hour trip from your place."

"What the hell am I transporting for that kind of money – plutonium?"

"All you got to know is that it's a package, and where and when it is to be delivered. You won't even have to touch it. Easy enough for 20 Gs."

"Twenty G's huh?"

"Yup. 20!"

"OK. I'm in."

"Good. Thanks. I appreciate it."

For the next few minutes, Syl filled *K* in on the specifics.

Sounded simple enough. But nothing worth that kind of money was simple. Drugs, guns? What? The money was just too good to pass up. So he did it.

Just like Syl promised, he never had to touch the package. It was delivered at night to his garage and loaded into his van. When he arrived at the dock at Lake Francis, it was the pilot who picked up the package and loaded it on the plane. Of course, by then it was obvious. The package wasn't drugs or guns. It was human.

Three days later *K* received another call from Syl.

"Good job, *K*. Package was delivered on time and undamaged. Appreciate it. The check is in the mail," he said with a mild chuckle. "Not to worry. You'll have it shortly."

"How you doin?" *K* asked just to be pleasant.

"Tell you the truth, not well. Not well. Doc says it's serious. Got a tumor on my liver. The size of Florida. They are going to operate but odds aren't great. Anyway, we'll see. Meanwhile, if I have more business to do on the side, can I call on you?"

"Sure, Syl. Sure. Whatever you need?" He almost sounded sincere.

"Thanks. Be talking to you."

K did one more job for Syl before he died. While they weren't bosom buddies, *K* respected him for the way he faced death. He accepted his fate. Didn't complain or ask forgiveness for all the sins he had committed. He was a fatalist to the end. But his end led *K* to all of this – for both good and bad.

A few days after Syl's death, *K* got a call from the guy who Syl worked for.

"Hello. Monsieur Knightsbridge?" The voice asked in a French accent.

"Speaking."

"My name is Lucien LeFreniere. I am ...or should I say...I was an associate of Sylvester Moore. An acquaintance of yours, I believe."

"Yes, I knew Syl. What can I do for you Mr. LeFreniere?"

"It is what we can do for each other."

"How so?"

"On two occasions you delivered sensitive packages for Monsieur Moore. Did you not?"

"Yes."

"Those packages were both for clients of mine. I respect the efficiency with which you accomplished the deliveries. With Monsieur Moore's passing, I will need someone that I can trust to provide similar services. Would you be interested?"

"For the money I was making, sure as hell would."

"Gratifying to hear such enthusiasm. I think that you will find your compensation even more lucrative without having to share the fee with Monsieur Moore."

That sonofabitch, *K* swore to himself. Syl was giving me only a portion of what was being paid for the transports.

"I'm sure I will," he answered calmly.

"Good. However, I would prefer concluding our arrangement in person. I will be briefly in Boston this Friday at the Logan Airport Hilton. Would you be available to meet with me, at 11?"

K agreed to the meet. He hung up the phone wondering where this would all lead.

■ ■ ■

The man opening the door to the suite was imposing. About 6'5", 250 lbs., and a head the size of a bowling ball cemented directly to a huge set of shoulders. His baldhead given an odd appearance by thick bushy eyebrows that joined above the bridge of his nose. Below the nose sprouted a thick brush of course black hair.

The man waved him into a large living room with magnificent panoramic views of the Boston skyline and harbor. Sitting on a leather coach at the far end of the room was a man whom Knightsbridge assumed was LeFreniere.

The Frenchman was trim and of average height. Looked like Robert Goulet if you could remember Robert Goulet when he was young. His thick, black hair was tinged with gray at the temples. He was wearing black slacks, leather Gucci loafers and a white silk shirt, unbuttoned at the top.

They shook hands and Goulet gestured for him to sit in one of the leather armchairs across from him.

"You may leave Hassan." He turned to *K*. "Imposing, isn't he?"

" 'Imposing' wouldn't be the word I'd use," *K* said with a grimace.

"My associate," LeFreniere said smiling. "He's Algerian and very devoted. Good to have men like that. You never know when they might be needed."

"Hopefully, he won't be needed," *K* said, rubbing his knees.

"I'm sure of that," LeFreniere responded, leaning back in his chair. "May I offer you some refreshment – coffee, espresso, tea, or perhaps, something stronger?"

"No, thanks. If you don't mind, I'd like to get on with this," K said, a bit too anxiously.

"You Americans! Always about the business. So, as you say, let us get on with this."

Leaning toward *K*, his hands outstretched, LeFreniere said, "Before agreeing to join our network, you must consider what I'm about to say. You must consider it very carefully. For this is a lifetime commitment. Once you join, you are ours. Do you wish me to continue?"

"By all means," he said apprehensively.

"Good. Then let me proceed. Everything I say from this point is for your ears only. You share it with no one. Comprendre?" This he said slowly and quietly, locking his penetrating dark brown eyes on *K's*. "Do you understand?"

K nodded that he did.

"I represent one in a group of networks that operates worldwide. We have a unique business model. Our market is the powerful, political, economic and social elite who have particular sexual desires. Desires with which you are familiar, I'm sure. To avoid exposure and the danger that naturally accompanies such perverse sexual proclivities, they require our assistance. The client places an order at a specific price with our organization. The order constitutes an RFP – a request for proposal. Any network that can fulfill the order to the client's satisfaction is rewarded the contract."

Perplexed, *K* asked the obvious, "How do you get chosen to fulfill the order?"

"Good question. Each client submits to the organization a detailed description of the sexual partner that they desire. Client orders are posted on our web site hidden deep in the Internet. It is unassailable except for those given the proper instructions. Individual operational groups – of which you may be one – then identify a prospective package that would fulfill the client's specifications. They post on the web site photographs and particulars of the boy or girl that fits the specifications. If there is a match, the operational unit receives the contract."

"Who sets the price of the contract?"

"The contract price is established by the organization."

"Does this organization have a name?"

"For lack of a better one, you may refer to us as the Illuminati."

"The what...?" K said with a confused expression.

"The Illuminati... the enlightened ones." LeFreniere said slowly with a touch of irritation.

Regrouping, K asked, "What's the take on my end?"

"That is also established by the organization and is non-negotiable but – and this is an important 'but' – it is always extremely lucrative for each member of a network. If I'm not mistaken, you have done quite well for your two deliveries."

"No argument there."

"So then, we begin, oui?"

"Oui."

"Bon! Bon!" LeFreniere stood and held out his hand. "I look forward to a long and lucrative association, monsieur Knightsbridge."

"Yes, me too."

With his forefinger to his lips, LeFreniere looked across at Knightsbridge.

"One other matter to be addressed before you leave. Monsieur Moore worked with an associate – a man named Donnelly. He was responsible for procuring the packages. You will need to replace him."

"Why? What happened to him?" Knightsbridge asked with some concern in his voice.

"Monsieur Donnelly was recently arrested and was found dead in his jail cell. Apparently, he hanged himself."

"Apparently?"

"De telles choses arrivent…Such things happen."

With a gesture toward the door, LeFreniere said, "Au revoir, monsieur Knightsbridge."

"Yah, goodbye," *K* said, a shiver running down his spine as he passed the Godzilla guarding the door.

As he walked through the open door, he turned and looked back at LeFreniere. "One other thing, sir. If I need to get in touch with you how do I do that?"

"Not to worry, Monsieur Knightsbridge. If there are problems, you will not have to contact us, we will contact you." A thin smile crossed LeFreniere's face as he feigned a weak wave goodbye.

That meeting seemed like only yesterday as he watched the Cessna slowly descend toward the glassy lake surface.

34

"We can't wait for backup," Ola whispered. "Another couple of minutes, they'll have those kids in the plane."

She turned to Leo, their faces so close they could feel each other's breath. "Work your way back across the road and approach from the woods on the left beyond where they've parked the van. I'll approach from here. I'll give you two minutes to get in position. Just be ready when I make my play. Be careful."

"You, too," he said moving off quickly to the other side of the access road.

Well, here goes nothing, she thought to herself. Ola waited the two minutes then stood up, emerging from the woods with her Glock in her right hand and her FBI identification in her left.

Ola walked directly at the two men who now stood at the rear of the van. "FBI," Ola shouted, "raise your hands and move away from the van. Now!"

The man in the leather coat suddenly dove behind the van while Clemmons turned and ran for the woods. Ola quickly ran to the side of the cabin. Kneeling down, she began scanning the van from left to right. Afraid of hitting any of the abducted children, she had to be careful about firing anywhere near the vehicle.

As these thoughts ran through her head, the perp broke for the dock with a gun in his hand. Turning, he fired off three rounds, attempting to keep Ola pinned behind the cabin.

Once he stopped firing, Ola leaned around the corner of the cabin, getting off two rounds. Her first was high but the next was on target. Though a bit low, the bullet struck just above his right buttocks, smashing the man's pelvis bone. He went sprawling headfirst into the dirt. On the ground moaning, he tried to roll on his side to return fire but the pain was fierce and his legs wouldn't respond.

Ola stood up and began walking toward the wounded suspect holding her gun steadily on him. As she approached, she heard the tat-tat-tat of an automatic weapon. She looked up to see flashes of light appear from the open cockpit of the plane. Multiple rounds sprayed around her kicking up dirt, pebbles and debris. Kneeling, she took careful aim at the gun flashes but before she could squeeze off a round she felt a hammer blow to her chest just above her left breast. The blow spun her around, landing her on her back. The air wheezed out of her chest and the blackness came.

■ ■ ■

Leo had made his way through the woods to the tree line opposite the stone retaining wall. He arrived just as Ola announced her presence to Clemmons and the guy in the leather coat. When he saw Clemmons turn and run for the tree line, he pushed himself against the trunk of an oak. Clemmons ran right toward him. Leo stuck out his right arm, clotheslining him. The guy dropped like a load of laundry.

Leo jumped on him, pressing his right knee against the small of Clemmons' back. He grabbed first the left arm securing it with one handcuff. He leaned over, "Get up," he hissed at Clemmons. Leo grabbed the man's belt and hauled him up pushing him hard, chest first against a young oak. He grabbed Clemmons' arms, pulled them around the tree and snapped the cuffs closed.

"Now stay put and keep your mouth shut," he warned Clemmons as he heard shots being fired. He turned and began running for the stonewall.

The FBI agent leaped over the wall, landing on a bed of stone that caused him to slip and fall into the shallow water. He got up quickly, his pants wet up to his crotch. Leaning against the retaining wall, Leo heard the fire of an automatic weapon. Peering over the wall he could see Ola. "God dammit," he cursed, "she's down."

Leo turned toward the open passenger door of the seaplane. First a foot slipped out the door onto a rung of the plane's ladder then he saw the short muzzle of an Uzi SMG. The shooter climbed out the door, his feet coming to rest on the pontoon with his back against the doorframe. He was scanning the area to see if anyone was with Ola.

As he turned to look down along the stonewall toward Leo, the agent took a deep breath, aimed and squeezed off three rounds from his Glock. His first bullet ricocheted off an airplane strut, but the second ripped into the pilot's shoulder and the third, proved a kill shot. It tore into his jugular, the severed artery releasing a stream of blood that gushed like water from a busted pipe. The fatally-wounded pilot fell onto the pontoon painting it crimson, then slowly rolled into the water, his life rapidly leaking away as a misty pink cloud in the lake water.

Leo hurriedly leaped over the stonewall and ran toward Ola, shouting her name. As he reached the fallen suspect still writhing in pain, he kicked the man's gun away from him, then dropped beside Ola's prostrate form.

"Ola, Ola, come on Ola. Talk to me, huh. Talk to me," he urged frantically. "Please don't die on me. Don't die, you hear me!"

Ola opened her eyes, looking at the tears welling up in Leo's. She put her hand to his face. "What a pussy you are," she whispered.

He took her up into his arms and hugged her tightly. She coughed, fighting for breath. "What are you trying to do, finish the job?"

"Sorry," he said, releasing his tight grip on her. "You are one lucky lady," fingering the hole in the Kevlar vest with the embedded slug. "A little higher and you wouldn't be getting up."

Ola reached out her arms to him and he lifted her up. She began to remove her vest gingerly. "Man that smarts," she cursed as she rubbed the spot where the slug had hit her vest.

She looked at Leo. "Did you get the bastard that shot me?"

"Yah, he's floating in the lake. I put one through his neck."

"Thanks, Leo."

"Next time, no Dirty Harry shit, OK?"

She smiled at him as he walked over to the wounded suspect. Leo knelt over him and whispered something in his ear. When Leo didn't get a response he pushed down with his left knee on the man's wound. He screamed with pain. "So," Leo said impatiently, "we goin' to do this again?"

Leo leaned closer to the man's mouth. He nodded as the man began answering his questions. "That's a good boy, we'll have help for you here shortly."

"So what did he give?" Ola asked.

"Where they were going."

"Which is…." She said drawing out the *is*.

"Halifax."

On cue, the back up arrived, both the New Hampshire State Police and the FBI agents. Leo called over to them indicating that he had a suspect cuffed in the woods behind the van and for them to call the paramedics.

Leo turned to Ola, ushering her with his hands toward the van, "Shall we see what he was delivering?"

Ola opened the doors at the rear of the van. There were two large zippered canvas bags. She opened one while Leo the other. She peeled the zipper down revealing the small, pale face of a young boy, no more than eight or nine years old. She lifted his eyelids. The pupils were dilated. He had been drugged. She felt for a pulse. Slow but steady. "Thank God. He's alive."

"I've got a small girl here, she seems OK too."

'We made the right call, Leo. Going in when we did. If we hadn't these kids would be gone now."

Ola looked toward the eastern sky in the direction from which the plane had come, her hands beginning to tremble uncontrollably.

35

As the entourage of ambulance and police vehicles arrived in front of the hospital's emergency entrance, the William Tell Overture rang out in the cab of the FBI SUV. With one hand on the steering wheel, Larry fumbled through his pockets searching for his cell.

"Ah, got it," he said taking the phone out of his inside jacket pocket. He looked at the screen and then at Bing. "Boss, it's Leo."

Bing took the phone. "Go in with Katie while I take this. See you in a minute."

"How'd it go?" Bing asked guardedly while watching them remove Katie from the ambulance. "You both OK?"

"Yah, Bing we're both OK though Ola caught one in her vest."

Bing winced, a sudden ripple of anxiety flashing across his chest. "What happened?"

Leo detailed what had occurred from the moment they arrived at the lake.

"So," Bing asked, "what kind of shape is our darling heroine in?"

"I think she's good to go. What do you have in mind?" Leo asked suspiciously rolling his eyes at Ola sitting on the edge of the ambulance.

"Let me speak to her first."

"Sure." Leo walked over to Ola and handed her the phone. "It's the boss."

Ola took the phone while rubbing her chest absent-mindedly. "Hi, Bingo," she said happily in an obvious attempt to avoid his sometimes overbearing, parental concern.

Bing instinctively knew what she was up to. "No bullshit, Ola. I need to know if you're able to continue in the field. You need to see a doctor, make sure that you don't have a broken rib or two, or a punctured lung or a..."

Ola interrupted his worst-of-all-cases scenarios before he could go ballistic on her. "Bingo, I'm fine. Hurts a little. That's all. Paramedic says I'm OK. So, where do we go from here?"

"You're being evasive. I can tell whenever you call me Bingo."

"Well I am OK, *Bing*," she responded.

"Fine, but this better not come back and bite the both of us in the ass!" There was silence on the phone for a moment.

"So Bingo, what's the plan?"

"The agents from Boston have interrogated Clemmons, whose real name, by the way, is Kent Knightsbridge. In the network he's known as *K*. Original, huh? He basically gave us everything we needed to know about how they plan to take the kidnap victims out of the country. From where you are, they were flying them to a chartered jet in Halifax, then on to Marseille. One of the agents sent from Boston is a pilot. The three of you are going to fly the next leg of the trip. Once in Nova Scotia, we'll have our Legal Attaché in Ottawa coordinate with the RCMP. Our legat in Paris will handle coordination in France. We're also applying for a yellow notice to Interpol to issue arrest warrants for those involved in this child abduction case. They'll also begin the coordination process with Europol and the law enforcement agencies of host countries. I want you to take this as far up the network as possible. If that means going to Marseille, then that's where you go. Parley vouz francais?"

"But Bingo," she said with false chagrin, "I have nothing to wear!"

"Yah, I know. That's what Leo is hoping." Bing heard a chuckle on the other end of the phone.

"And, one more thing. Clemmons – I mean Knightsbridge – also gave the boys some good intel on how they manage the network. These guys use a site in the deep web."

"What the hell is the deep web?"

"Without getting into specifics, it's the part of the web that hardly anyone visits, unless you know where you're going and how to get there. You can think of the entire web as one giant iceberg with one percent above the surface. That is where most of us surf but the other 99 percent is hidden beneath the surface. You can't get there without the right software and know how. That's how the network manages command and control of their system."

"Sounds Orwellian."

"Our cyber geeks at Quantico are working on finding and breaking into the site. If they do that, we have a treasure trove of intel. I'll keep you informed. Their intel could be key in destroying the network."

"Thanks for the tutorial. Got to go now."

"Incidentally, remember, that the two of you are going overseas as *observers*. The host countries' national police forces will take the lead. And..." he hesitated, "both of you ... be safe."

Just as Bing hung up, the cell rang again. "Yup," he said dully. "SSA Ingram here."

"Hi Bing. It's Martha Tompkins, public information in the Boston field office."

"Hi Martha. I remember you from that case a few months back. How are you?"

"Fine. Hope you are too after what you've been through today. Congrats, by the way. Just calling as a heads up. The press is going to be swarming the hospital in about 10 minutes. I'm having the locals keep them in the ER parking lot. I suggest you let them cool their heels for about 20 minutes or so and then give them a brief news conference. I don't have time to get there to assist, so this is all on you."

Bing began to rub his lower lip and then his brow as he felt the mother of all headaches coming on. "So what do I say and how do I say it?"

"You know, the usual." She took a deep breath. "Introduce and thank everyone. Provide an update on the girl's overall condition. No specifics. Leave that to the MD. You can indicate

arrests made and fatalities but again, no specifics. We'll handle
that once we have all our ducks in a row. Also, allude to the fact
that this is an ongoing investigation so you can't share much.
Let them know that we'll be holding a follow-up briefing in
our Boston field office tomorrow afternoon, time to be deter-
mined. My suggestion, make it short and sweet, and then get
the hell out of there."

"You sound like my last girl friend. Thanks, Martha. I'll let
you know how it goes."

He dropped the cell into his pocket thinking about Ola and
Leo, and how far up the line they would get. Maybe Ola was
right. Maybe there is an Illuminati.

The news conference went as well as he could have hoped.
Bing didn't like doing these public kinds of things but it came
with the territory. He wouldn't believe it, but the people around
him thought he was an excellent presenter. His bosses at the
FBI always preferred putting him up front because he handled
the media well and he made such a good, reassuring presence.

He followed the general script laid out by Martha but
took special pains to recognize the efforts of his team, and
the Wilton and Massachusetts State Police. He also singled out
Trish for the exceptional and professional job she did as first
responder. Though he knew that she was slightly embarrassed
by the praise, he could also see that she beamed with pride.

Finally, Bing singled out two others for praise.

"We couldn't have rescued Katie as quickly as we did without the courageous efforts of two neighborhood dogs, Shelly
and Bosco. They tracked the abductor and Katie from shortly

after she was abducted until her rescue. In fact, it was the dogs intervention that probably saved her life and eventually led to the abductor's death. Both are now being treated for some wounds suffered while protecting Katie. We all owe a debt of gratitude to those brave dogs."

The crowd of media types began hurling questions at him like Molotov cocktails. "I'm sorry you'll have to wait a few days before the dogs are well enough to answer your questions." He deadpanned as a ripple of laughter erupted among them. "Remember, this is an ongoing investigation. We should have more for you tomorrow at the formal FBI briefing in Boston."

The last thing Bing did at the impromptu news conference was to allow the Gaines to speak briefly. They were, naturally, effusive in the praise of everyone involved, especially Bing and the dogs – Shelly and Bosco.

■ ■ ■

Fitzi and Arnie Cook were standing next to each other behind Bing during the news conference. As it wrapped up, the Wilton Police Chief nudged Fitzi in the ribs. "Hey, you never told me what the hell Bing meant when he said 'It was beauty killed the beast.'"

Fitzi smiled incredulously at Chief Cook. "You're not much of a moviegoer are you?"

"I wouldn't say that. I see my fair share. What has that got to do with anything?"

"You see chief," nodding his head toward Bing, "he's a guy that loves to salt his talk with literary and movie allusions. Don't you know the movie that line comes from?"

"What line? Yah mean 'It was beauty killed the beast?' "

"Yes, that's what I mean," he said rolling his eyes. "You ever see *King Kong*?"

"Sure, when I was a kid."

"Well, in the final scene the movie producer, Carl Denham, is standing next to a dead Kong at the foot of the Empire State Building. A police lieutenant next to him says, 'Well, Denham, the airplanes got him.' Denham replies, 'Oh no, it wasn't the airplanes. It was beauty killed the beast.' Quite apropos, don't you think?"

The Chief lifted his cap and scratched his balding head. "So what Bing is saying is that it wasn't the dogs but his going after this pretty little girl that killed him." Fitzi pointed his forefinger at him – "Bingo!"

"I tell yah," the Chief muttered, "Bing is a helluva police officer but he sure is an odd duck."

"Yeah, but one smart odd duck!"

■ ■ ■

With the media briefing concluded, Bing made his way through the crowd back through the ER and a set of swinging doors into a long corridor. Halfway down, he dropped himself onto a bench. Resting his elbows on his knees he put his head in his hands.

He looked up as the doors swung open and Trish came walking toward him. She sat down placing her arm around his shoulders. "What's wrong?" she said sympathetically. "What are you thinking about?"

Bing was always amazed at how quickly women became atuned to people's moods. He looked at her and she stared back intently. "Tell me," she said not as a command but rather as permission.

He smiled slightly. "I was just thinking of the one young girl that I didn't save."

"But you saved this one."

"No, I didn't. The dogs did that," he said ruefully.

She stroked his cheek gently. "You expect too much of yourself." She watched as his Adam's apple moved slightly. "You're a great cop and a good man."

She moved her face gently toward his then lightly touched her lips to his. The kiss was wet, soft, alluring. As she slowly began to pull away he stopped her. "No," Bing commanded quietly, pulling her closer, their lips meeting with more force, more passion, more promise.

36

Over the next few days Katie, Shelly and Bosco became media stars. They first appeared on local Boston TV and then they had appearances on CNN with Wolf Blitzer and the Ellen DeGeneres Show. Word was that they also had been scheduled to appear on 60 Minutes. While the power couple of Tom and Giselle did get a brief appearance on CNN, they became lost in the publicity backwash. Such is the fickle nature of media fame.

Bing and Trish had their first date. And while Bing insisted that she'd make a great FBI agent and that he'd recommend her for the academy, she demurred. "I like Wilton, and besides, having a career as an FBI agent isn't high on my priority list." What is? He had asked.

"Foolish, man," she had replied. "You, of course!"

■ ■ ■

Working with Interpol's international sex trafficking task force, the RCMP, Europol, and the French Police Nationale, Ola and Leo had been successful, bringing down the network from New Hampshire to Marseille. There the trail dried up until Ola received a call from Quantico.

"Hello, Special Agent Dabrowski. My name is Joe Huberhoff. I'm in cyber forensics at Quantico. SSA Ingram asked me to call and brief you on what we've found in the deep web site you folks put us on to."

Huberhoff spent the next 15 minutes briefing Ola. "The site would have been extremely difficult to find if it hadn't been for the search key that came from you guys," he explained.

"What was the key?" Ola asked.

"Yah see, these sites floating in the deep web don't actually sit there waiting to be visited ..." he began to explain.

"OK." Ola interrupted, becoming exasperated with Huberhoff the techno geek. "So cut to the chase for me, please."

"But it's so interesting. Here's the bottom line ... these sites are dynamically created whenever you begin a search using the right key word or phrase. Once we did a search for that word – presto – it magically appeared."

"Great," Ola said with some degree of irritation. "What was the search key?"

"Funny you should ask that. It was the name of the guy who founded the Illuminati back in 1776. His name was Adam Weishaupt. Odd, huh?"

"No, not really. Thanks for your help, Hooper."

"No, mam, it's Huberhoff, my name, that is."

"Good, you remember that. Ciao!"

Leo was standing next to her listening. "That was cold," he whispered. "Something bothering you?"

"Sorry," she offered lamely. "I just can't stop thinking of all the kids who have disappeared, maybe dead. Its just too much to deal with."

"Hey, I handle it by just not thinking about it. If I did, I'd probably just go out and hurt somebody."

Ola looked at Leo knowingly. *Not true Leo, you think about them, you're too good of a guy not to.*

With the techno geek's intel they now had enough info to follow the trail directly to the man who placed the order to take Katie. The intel sent them off first to Cairo and then on to the United Arab Emirates.

In each country the local FBI legat had coordinated the operation with local and national police forces. When they arrived in Abu Dhabi, members of the General Directorate of Police met them. They were led by Colonel Faris El-Amin, commander of the Criminal Investigation Department. After meeting the Colonel, Ola thought that the locals must consider this a very high profile and sensitive case. He was friendly but business-like, and just a bit nervous. Their next stop was the headquarters of the International Bank of the United Arab Emirates to find the man who had placed the order for Katie.

■ ■ ■

Mahmood sat at his desk with his cell in his hand. He had bad news to deliver to Samir and the Sheikh. His hand trembled slightly. This would not be easy. His world had begun to collapse only a few hours ago while sitting in the rear of his Lexus limo heading along Hazza Bin Zayed. The traffic had been, as always, heavy and congested. It had given him the time to review the file of a very rich and successful contractor from Dubai. This client would require his undivided attention for the next week or so. Much to do to organize his portfolio. These thoughts evaporated into the Lexus's chilled air when next to him his cell phone began to buzz and hop like a Mexican jumping bean.

Mahmood's anxiety level skyrocketed as he saw who was calling. He raised the cell to his ear. "Allo, Monsieur LeFreniere."

"Mahmood, don't have much time. The package has been interdicted. The network has been compromised all the way to Marseille. They will be here shortly. Take all due precautions, destroy everything! No further contact unless we contact you. The site will also be going dark. Good luck."

■ ■ ■

With that call out of the way, LeFreniere made another. This one would be more difficult. The man at the other end was perhaps the most dangerous man he knew, capable of delivering unspeakable pain to those who failed him. But, like LeFreniere, he was a member of the Illuminati Circle and so protocol required this call.

"Hello," LeFreniere said hesitatingly, "I have bad news."

"News? What's this news, Francuz!" The other voice mumbled with a discernable Slavic accent in nearly unintelligible English. Another reason LeFreniere hated talking to him. LeFreniere couldn't speak Polish and the Pole couldn't speak French. English was the only recourse, but the Pole's was atrocious.

"The network has been seriously compromised."

"Who does this?"

"Police. Interpol. French National Police and… the Americans, I think."

"Amerykanie?! Why?"

"Don't know," he lied, knowing full well why the Americans might be involved. "I'm just calling to alert you. I must leave now. Will contact you when it is safe to do so."

"Where you go?"

"Don't want to say over the phone. I'll be in touch."

"You listen, Francuz! Don't go far or we find you."

"I won't. Suggest you do the same. Au revoir, mon ami."

LeFreniere shut off the disposable cell. He reached into his desk and retrieved his Israeli Jericho semi-automatic. With the gun's butt he smashed the cell, throwing the pieces into a wastebasket. He tucked the gun into his waist belt.

"Hassan," he called out to the open office door, "get in here."

The Algerian giant walked into the office. "Oui, monsieur."

"We go, now. Throw some clothes together and get the Mercedes out front in five minutes. Do it," he said, making a hurried arm gesture toward the door.

LeFreniere grabbed a small leather valise, loading it with desk files, a laptop and a half dozen disposable cell phones. Before leaving he went to a closet and retrieved a small overnight bag with two changes of clothes and toiletries – his get-out-of-town-in-a-damned-hurry bag.

Under the bag was a small safe. He opened it and retrieved a half million Euro. Enough to last him for a while.

He made one last reconnaissance of the room. Satisfied, he set the switch, giving himself three minutes. He ran down the stairs, taking them two at a time, flying through the glass doors and flinging himself into the Mercedes back seat.

"Get us out of here," he yelled to Hassan. A hundred yards down the street an explosion ripped through the waterfront neighborhood, spreading debris in a wide arc as the Marseille Transshipping building erupted in a ball of flame.

LeFreniere never looked back.

■ ■ ■

Pushing back in his desk chair, Mahmood reluctantly placed the call to Samir.

"Allo, Mahmood. Good to hear from you. I was thinking of calling for an update on our package."

"That's why I'm calling, Samir," pausing for a moment and clearing his throat, Mahmood continued, "the package cannot be delivered."

"What are you saying Mahmood? Why not?" He said, a high degree of alarm in his voice.

"The package has been interdicted by the authorities. The network has been compromised. We can do nothing further for the foreseeable future. This has to be the last time we have any communication regarding this business. Is that clear?"

"What is clear, Mahmood, is that you owe the Sheikh $1.25 million and that this matter has to end with you. Do you take my meaning, Mahmood?" His voice was cold and menacing. "This matter must stop with you. If the authorities get to you they must get no further. Do you understand what I'm saying, Mahmood? No further than you. If the Sheikh or I should be compromised then your family will have no one to ensure their safety and security. Their lives and their futures are in your hands, mon ami. Do not fail us!"

"I understand completely. Assure the Sheikh that his money will be refunded and this business ends with me. Goodbye, Samir" he said with finality.

Mahmood dropped the cell phone on his desk, got up from his chair, walked over to the buffet and poured himself a very large Glenrothes. He swallowed it in one continuous gulp. As he looked out over the azure blue bay he could only curse himself for becoming involved in such a disgusting business. But that, after all, was what it was all about – business!

■ ■ ■

Mahmood thought back to a time when all seemed right with his world. He felt in absolute control, a sheikh ruling over a vast financial domain. En route to the bank one April morning eight years ago, the personal wealth account manager had received a call from his uncle, Sheikh Abdulla Al Dahliri. the senior executive vice president and second most powerful executive at the bank, had asked to see Mahmood in his palatial office on the bank's 20th floor. It was a rarified place seldom visited by the likes of Mahmood. This invitation portended either very good or very bad news. He began to sweat.

As the elevator door opened on the 20th floor, Mahmood ran his index finger inside the collar of his heavily starched white shirt. The heat seemed intolerable. He took a deep breath, stopped a moment before the glass office doors, and quietly focused on maintaining his composure. After all, what was to fear? He had performed extremely well in his role as a personal wealth manager. All his clients appeared to be very satisfied with his performance and service. Nothing, absolutely nothing could be wrong, so why be so fearful? The answer to the why, of course, lay on the other side of the glass doors.

Entering the office suite he was greeted by his uncle's personal secretary, a demur but stunningly attractive woman, evidently European or … American? She nodded to Mahmood. "As-salam alaykum." Mahmood nodded slightly returning the greeting.

"Follow me, please. Your uncle's office is down this corridor," she indicated to her right. He followed her, forgetting momentarily the fear and anxiety he was experiencing, as he watched her slender and supple figure ripple rhythmically under her gossamer-like dress.

She opened a large glass door to an enormous office suite. "Your uncle is expecting you," she said, glancing over to the far corner to a large glass table behind which sat the Sheikh.

Mahmood attempted rather awkwardly to approach his uncle with some degree of confidence. The Sheikh was dressed formally in a brilliant white dishdash and keffyeh, fastened about his head with a black cord. The cord was a reminder of his tribe's Bedouin ancestors who used the agal as a tether for their camels.

Sensing Mahmood's anxiety, the Sheikh stepped out from behind the desk. "Mahmood, Mahmood! Why look so grim? I am your uncle, we are family after all," he exclaimed, grabbing Mahmood by the shoulders and placing a kiss on both cheeks.

"Come my nephew, sit with me." The Sheikh, grabbing the sides of his billowing thobe, sat down at the end of a large, plush sofa facing a magnificent panorama of downtown Abu Dhabi. He gestured to Mahmood to take a seat next to him. "Is this not a most lovely view of our wonderful city, Mahmood?"

"Yes, it is sir. Very beautiful." Mahmood was feeling and sounding more comfortable. His uncle would not be planting kisses if the news were bad. "May I ask uncle, why have you extended me this invitation to visit?"

"Mahmood, my boy. Cannot an uncle ask to see his nephew? Yes?" he laughed. "But it is typical of you to get right down to business. So to business it is."

The Sheikh leaned back against the couch, his hands clasped together.

"Naturally, I have been following your progress here at the bank. I must say that I have been very impressed. So have other members of our management team. I have said as much to your very proud parents. In fact, you have performed so well, that we wish to promote you to a more senior position. One where we can more fully enjoy the fruits of your labor and the acumen of that brilliant financial mind of yours," smiling as he pressed a finger lightly against Mahmood's forehead.

The look of shock on Mahmood's face brought a wide grin to the Sheikh's. "What's the matter my boy, did you expect a demotion for excellent performance?" He slapped Mahmood on the knee then took his nephew's hand in both of his and shook it vigorously. "So congratulations, Mahmood. I know that you will do an excellent job for us."

The Sheikh leaned back stretching his arms over the back of the couch. "Naturally, this promotion comes with a considerable increase in responsibility. You will be managing all of the personal account managers with clients in the Emirates. If all goes well, then I can see a senior vice presidency in your future...and who knows, perhaps president. We need good, young blood like yours in our leadership."

Mahmood sat there in a state of disbelief. This was far more than he had ever hoped for. Jamillah would be deliriously happy and so very proud. "I do not know what to say uncle. I am so very honored."

The Sheikh put his hand on Mahmood's shoulder. "Nonsense my boy, nonsense. You deserved everything we have given you – which reminds me. There is a significant increase in compensation. You will also enjoy stock options based on performance and your choice of automobiles and a personal chauffeur. No more wasting time driving into work on these congested roadways. No, not for our new vice president. Eh?"

Then the Sheikh stood up, resting his folded hands on the slight paunch of his stomach. His expression became suddenly drawn. "There is one sensitive item, however, that we must discuss before you accept this position." Mahmood's face quickly began to fade from ecstasy to worry, as if a shade had been lowered.

The Sheikh began to walk back and forth in front of Mahmood, struggling for how best to broach the subject.

"Mahmood, I know how acutely aware you are of the paramount importance we place on satisfying our customers. How do the western management gurus put it 'do not just meet, but exceed expectations.' Well, that is what you have done so effectively and efficiently. You have made your clients extremely happy. But as vice president you will have your own portfolio of very, and I mean, very important and very rich clients. Their needs – *desires*, if you will – and not just financial, however odd or bizarre, must be attended to. Some of these desires may be considered beyond the scope of our talents. They may be somewhat disagreeable. Nevertheless, as you know, we must do all we can to satisfy our clients. Let me be plain with you, Mahmood. We have a group of clients – a very special, few, to be sure – who have *unusual* sexual appetites. Some like boys, some like girls, and some like them young … very young. Procuring such is often difficult, not to mention dangerous, even for the rich and powerful."

The Sheikh paused for a moment, examining Mahmood's face.

"Of course, the bank is not, nor will it ever be in the procurement business. No, we leave that disgusting business to others. However, to keep our clients hands as clean as possible, we have access to a network. A service if you will, that can for a price, procure a sexual partner of any age, gender or description that our client demands. Access to this service has been placed in the hands of one and only one of our vice presidents. So secretive and so sensitive is its use. For years it was my responsibility and then that of your predecessor's until his untimely death. Now, if you accept this position, it will be yours."

The Sheikh sat down next to Mahmood looking him in the eye. "So, what say you Mahmood? Are you willing to take on this awesome responsibility?"

Mahmood turned away for a moment. He knew his decision would be a fateful one. What would Allah say? But then again, was it not Allah who put him here in this place? Perhaps Mahmood was the best man to oversee such a service to mitigate, to whatever extent possible, its harm. No, this was all moral gymnastics. If he accepted, he did so knowing that it would be a cruel and foul business – but the rewards – the rewards!

"I don't know my uncle. I think of the children that will suffer. It is a nasty business."

"Yes, Mahmood, it is. But these are not our children. They are not Allah's children. We protect our own, our families, our friends. What happens to nonbelievers is not our concern. Do you know your haditha, Mahmood?"

"I have studied my Qur'an. I am familiar."

"Well good. If you may recall…. *'I heard Allah's Messenger saying, Everyone of you is a guardian, and responsible for what is in his custody. The ruler is a guardian of his subjects and responsible for them; a husband is a guardian of his family and is responsible for it; a lady is a guardian of her husband's house and is responsible for it, and a servant is a guardian of his master's property and is responsible for it. I heard that from Allah's Messenger and I think that the Prophet also said, A man is a guardian of his father's property and is responsible for it, so all of you are guardians and responsible for your wards and things under your care.'"*

"Think upon these words, Mahmood? Time is short."

Mahmood stood sitting, his face in his hands. He knew in the deepest quiet of his being that his uncle was distorting the teachings of the Prophet. He believed in a kind, loving and accepting Allah who would never countenance the harming of an innocent, believer or not. But uncle was a deceiver – one who deceived himself as he readily as he deceived others.

Though Mahmood knew all this to be true, his decision had been made. To deny his uncle's offer would be to bring an end to his rise among the bank's power elite. He had worked so hard, given up so much to earn this opportunity. He could not, must not squander it now.

Mahmood looked up, turning his face toward the Sheikh. "Yes, I will take the position. For my family, for Jamillah and Baseema." Mostly, though left unspoken, he would take it for himself.

The Sheikh slapped him on the back. "Good, my boy! I hoped you would accept. And I know that you will have great success. Now let me have Haifa show you to your new offices." He got on the intercom with his secretary. "Mahmood will be out shortly. Could you please show him to his new offices? Thank you."

He turned to Mahmood. "Lovely, girl, Haifa, is she not? I named her *Haifa* because she was so slender and she still is but … not all over," he laughed lightly. "She was procured for me when she was only 12. My lover until I sent her off to college. Now look at her. A wonderful assistant. As commanded by the Prophet Muhammad, may the mercy and blessings of God be upon him, I protect her now because she is my ward and I am her guardian. So, we are not so cruel after all, are we Mahmood?"

That was the day Mahmood began this unspeakable business as a member of the Illuminati Circle.

■ ■ ■

Mahmood worked fast now to destroy all documentation of his association with the network and to prepare his finances to ensure Jamillah's and Baseema's futures. They were all he had left.

For the rest of the day he shredded documents, including anything relating to Samir or the Sheikh. When he finished with the shredding, he began to review his finances. He now regretted not making his wife and daughter privy to the web of personal accounts and investments that he had accumulated and managed over the years. Then, again, if he had, they would have naturally questioned him on the source of many of the large deposits that funded much of their personal wealth. Questions that he knew he could not or would not answer. They would have difficulty understanding and accepting all of this.

Mahmood sat back down at his desk and began to type on his laptop detailed instructions to his personal solicitor. The instructions identified a file attachment that was a complete record of all his personal finances. He provided information on the location of the funds. How they should be disbursed. The level of control that should be given to his wife and daughter. And a minimum yearly income that they should receive. He also named a wealth management firm in Switzerland, where one of his British classmates from the London School of Economics was a vice president, as both custodians and managers of his extensive holdings.

Mahmood ran off a copy of the letter of instructions, signed it, placed it in an envelope, and addressed it. He thought it to sensitive to email. He called in Haseena and asked her to send the envelope by private courier. He dropped back down into his chair, emotionally and physically spent

Two days had passed and Mahmood was feeling a bit more comfortable. Maybe they wouldn't make the connection to him. Perhaps the trail ended with LeFreniere in Marseille. Wishful thinking perhaps. But as each day passed he became more and more hopeful.

He had been occupying his mind, distracting himself from the devastating possibilities that loomed before him. The hours had been preoccupied of late with the financial life of his most recent client. A man with more pies than he had fingers. His was a rabbit warren of tangled financial arrangements and investment skullduggery. It would challenge the acumen and mental stability of many a wealth manager. Nevertheless, he pushed forward, not so much because the personal wealth of the client topped 100 million US, but because it was a grateful distraction until…

…the intercom rang. Reluctantly, with trembling hand, he picked it up. "Mr. Mahmood. Some men are here to see you."

"Who are they, Haseena?"

"Well, sir, I believe they are all with the police. There is a Colonel with three officers of the Abu Dhabi CID, an inspector from Interpol, and three agents from the FBI in the U.S."

"What do they want with me?" he asked with an unconvincing sense of bravado.

"They need to speak with you about an urgent police matter. That's all they said."

"Please give me a few moments before you usher them in."

Mahmood knew what he had to do. It must stop here. For the welfare of the bank, but, most importantly, for the welfare of his family. They'll understand that he did it for them.

Mahmood placed his face into his hands bending his head in supplication. In a low voice barely audible, he began recitation of a du'a for forgiveness.

"*Subhanakal lahomma wabihamdik. Ash-hado alla-ilaha-illa ant. Astaghfiroka w'atoobo-ilayk* ... Glory be to You, Oh Allah, and all praise! I testify that there is no deity but You. I seek Your forgiveness and to You I do repent."

Three times he recited his du'a. Three times he repented for all the sins that he had committed.

Reaching into the middle draw of his desk he removed an envelope in light blue vellum addressed to his wife and daughter. He then removed his personal Berretta from the lower right hand drawer. He gingerly fingered the note to his family, a last touching goodbye, placed the barrel of the Berretta into his mouth and squeezed the trigger. *Extreme sanction!*

Everyone in the outside vestibule jumped when the gun went off. Ola and Colonel El- Amin were closest to Mahmood's office door. As they rushed in weapons drawn, they could see his head lying on the desk, a large river of blood slowly flowing over the rich leather veneer and pooling against a tall pile of paper files. Behind him the expansive panoramic view of the Khor al Bateen was obscured by the splatter of blood, brain, skull and skin fragments, ever so slowly dripping down to the windowsill.

Ola moved to the side of the body. No need to check for a pulse with a golf-ball size hole in the back of his head. Near his right hand, she could see an envelope addressed to Jamillah and Beseema. She grabbed a letter opener from his desk caddy and carefully lifted the envelope from the growing pool of blood, placing it on top of the pile of papers. "Who are Jamillah and Baseema?" she asked of no one in particular.

"They are his wife and daughter," from the doorway, Haseena offered with moist eyes, "such a lovely family."

Ola looked at the secretary. If only he had been thinking of his family, Ola thought, before he had arranged the abduction of an 11-year-old American girl and who knows how many others.

EPILOGUE

Bing was rifling through a pile of files when his office door opened. "We're baaaack!" said a grinning Leo with Ola following behind him.

"Jeez, great to see the both of you. Welcome back and great job out there. The director was mightily impressed."

"Should be. We bagged a whole shit load of scumbags," Leo grinned. "Last count, must have been 23 and they're not finished yet!"

"And how are you holding up, Ola?" Bing asked with concern in his voice.

"I'm fine, Bing. But I do need to redo my wardrobe if we're going on any more of these European junkets. The French guys were hot!"

"You might just have your wish, Ola." Bing bent his head to see around the pair into the doorway. "Is Larry lurking outside there?"

"Here boss," Larry chimed, peering around the corner of the door.

"Well, good. Now that I have you all here, I've received our next assignment. The director has designated our CARD team to be part of an international task force on child sex trafficking. Seems we've developed some kind of international rep for this kind of investigatory work. Anyway, we begin on Wednesday, so get your passports in order."

"Geez, boss," Larry sighed. "Don't we even get a few days to wallow in the praise and admiration of our compadres for the job we've just done?"

"Sorry, Larry, but maybe I can make it up to all of you. How about joining a friend and me for dinner at Erbaluce's tonight?" Noticing some hesitation, he added, "Named best Italian restaurant in Boston. I'll buy!" 'The I'll buy' was the closer.

"Be still my heart," Ola exclaimed, then pausing a minute, she looked at Bing knowingly. "This friend wouldn't be a hottie from Wilton, would it?"

"La maniere intelligente de vous, mon ami!"

Bing stood up smiling, grabbing the thickest of the folders on his desk. He handed it to Ola. "Here, all three of you should familiarize yourself with this report. Get it back to me tomorrow. Now, on to Erbaluce's. Trish is joining us there at 6:30."

As Bing walked toward the elevator, the three agents hung back a bit as Ola opened the file with both Larry and Leo peering over her shoulder. She snapped her index finger under the Interpol Threat Assessment subject line, smiling at the guys. "I told you so!"

It read: *International Child Sex Trafficking and the Illuminati Circle.*

Made in the USA
Columbia, SC
20 November 2017